The Scream of Feyer

CW01020006

By Steve Hammond Kaye

WARNING

This book contains graphic scenes of <u>sex</u>, <u>violence</u> and <u>horror</u>. It is NOT suitable for minors.

If you have painful memories of <u>abortion</u>, <u>genocide</u>, <u>rape</u> and /or <u>bombings</u>, then please <u>DO NOT</u> read this book.

STANDARDCUTMEDIA

Copyright Notice

Published in 2013 in the UK by:

STANDARDCUTMEDIA
International House
39 Great Windmill Street
LONDON
W1D 7LX
www.standardcut.co.uk
publishing@standardcut.co.uk

A catalogue record of this book is available from the British Library.

ISBN 13: 978-0957479524
ISBN 10: 0957479522

THE SCREAM OF FEVER

To my great friend
George. A book to light
your dark fires with the
coals of shaded intimacy.
Very few would understand this
book George, but it is made
for a small elite of survivors
and you my friend are numbered
in that elite. Thank you for
creating my spirit — enjoy.

STEVE HAMMOND KAYE

Dedicated to Nicholas Kirkby

My soul brother.

table of contents

Thirty Four Minutes Dead

The prequel to *The Scream of Feyer*

Gregory Vain, a pioneering neurosurgeon and part of **'The Memory-Camera Project'** is part of a pioneering team that develops the ability to unlock the frozen images stored within the cortex of the dead mind and to read the living, thinking brain. He must also fend-off erotic advances from the vampirical Marcia Levene to save his marriage.

Steve Hammond Kaye's neo-gothic techno-thriller of power, knowledge, violence, treachery and blood-lust enjoy the paginated battleground in this dystopian vision of the near future - *Thirty Four Minutes Dead...*

Thirty Four Minutes Dead
The prequel to *The Scream of Feyer*

She'll laugh at your fire…, burn in your fire…, die in your fire…

prologue

A thin ethereal mist still clung to the lower reaches of the valley, although the sun had risen an hour earlier. Feyer stirred and brushed the dew from her naked svelte frame.

She pulled on her ragged clothes and then scanned her immediate surroundings. The woman knew that she was still in the valley lowlands, but the rest were not in sight. Her separation had been deliberate, giving her privacy to contemplate her situation.

Feyer had last menstruated ten weeks hence and it looked as though sex that way had cost her dear. She had wanted to feel semen surge through her vagina again and now she was rueing her self-indulgence.

Feyer had waited so long. Like the other women she had helped make the rules and thus she knew that penetrative sex was only allowed via the mouth or anus. She knew that this made sense, understanding that any pregnancy would slow the Avoiders down or worse – break their cover. The woman knew that she was pregnant and she acknowledged what she must do to rectify the situation. Feyer reached for her provisions bag and selected two old metal knitting needles so she could implement the necessary action.

She lowered her jeans, but left her ragged briefs on. Feyer positioned the needles into a crevice

between the tightly packed rocks nearby and she then impaled herself on the twin prongs. The woman didn't make a sound as her blood re-coloured the basalt rock face.

This was Feyer's antidote to her own wayward indulgence. Her womb would carry nothing now, as she had undertaken her task with a savage resolution. She straightened and started to walk back down the trail, to where her fellow Avoiders would be located. Her blood left her scent and her maternal instincts were solidified red – left out to dry and die. Feyer glanced at the valley and quietly spoke to her world.

"Fuck creation. You stagnant wasteland."

Bones of a Madman by Justin Mason

one

The crowd started queuing at eight that morning. They knew that the bread lorry would arrive sometime in the next four hours. It always did.

There was no jostling, no contention surrounding the placement order, nothing to break the uniform obedience to the *Prerogative Three* instructions that set their ordered lives in motion.

A gentle wind blew down the Main Street and the faces turned to catch the cool air. The litter spread through the throng, encircling the heels of those in attendance like a missing ingredient to complete the vagrant package.

A child let out a faint cry, not for frustration or anger and not for temper or discontent. The cry was determined by hunger, a necessity that had been kept in place. Hunger was not a threatening emotional state; just a physical need and they had allowed retention for purely pragmatic reasons.

A lean mongrel distracted the infant and it reached out to touch the dog. This spontaneous movement caused the child to fall from the broken sidewalk and it fell quite heavily on its knees. The child began to laugh and the mother echoed the laughter with her head held aloft to the Washington sky. This reaction prompted a ripple of laughter from those around the pair and the amusement spread through the ranks like an automated chain-reaction. The infant struggled to its feet with one knee bleeding profusely. It smiled,

11

starting to laugh again.

At just after eleven, the bread lorry arrived being driven at high speed, frequently touching the edge of the sidewalk. One woman was standing just on the edge and the vehicle cut her down before arriving at the Distribution point.

The driver released a wry smile. He had been an MC-Project employee for a decade, but hitting one on the edge gave him as much pleasure now as it always had.

To him the perks had been quite advantageous. He hadn't been subjected to Prerogative Three modification and he had a vocation that never seemed to dry up.

He had eased into the surf-line perks that the other drivers shared with him and edge- trimming was second only to the carnal privileges that the position offered him. He knew that after the bread was supplied through the line, he could take any female, enjoy his chosen pleasures and then discard the selected femme in any of the outskirt disposal sites. Unlike some of the other drivers, he never chose the release-option, preferring to retain novelty in each of his selections.

"He'll chose the mother Dave. You can tattoo my labia if I'm wrong!"

Tavini waited, not responding to Levene's challenge. He had been proved wrong in their high-rise vantage point too many times before.

"Knew it Dave. Driver 26 is always prone to blonde selections!"

The MC-Project pair enjoyed verbal sparring, remaining unperturbed by the felled female or the *snatch* of the blonde mother by Driver 26. The child was left alone as the crowd filed away with diminished smiles on their faces and low-grade baguettes in their hands. Tavini and Levene had

watched the events unfold after the bread lorry had arrived. On floor twenty-nine, they were enjoying their sport before they would turn their attention to serious Memory-Camera Project business. The pair didn't have any feelings for the vagrant throng below them. Their *advanced* brains had the capacity to care, but any inclination for this moral trait was discarded like spittle on the sidewalk.

"Are you briefing the Avoider state of play at the noon meet Marcia?"

"Yeah. All the main MC-Project players will be in attendance and I'm on first, after Mr Wheeler's introduction."

As Levene straightened her posture to move away from the window David Tavini saw a chance to arrest her forward motion, locking her frame with his sizeable athletic arms.

"Those damned Driver hits always turn you on don't they Mr Tavini?"

"For sure. I guess Driver 26 is still the ultimate poacher in my mind. I mean the guy springs on his women like a released wild animal! He knows that the distribution crowds have been through the Prerogative Three alterations and don't have the capacity to resist his manic advances, but he still gets pumped on some kind of depraved male savagery! A few weeks back when you were assessing Avoider activity in Europe, the guy sprang on one woman with such ferocity that he broke her fucking neck! She was mortuary-meat in a split second!"

Marcia Levene let Tavini bend her over her favourite black power-chair. She wondered what her MC-Project colleague had in mind for their mutual satisfaction purposes. *Objects* were Tavini's favourite sexual indulgence and the woman had become quite accustomed to his inventive selections. The pair had only rarely copulated because Levene had other partners for that express purpose and Tavini preferred voyeurism to penetrative sex. Despite these different preferences, they would achieve mutual sexual satisfaction by indulging in Sado-Masochism before MC-Project meetings. Tavini usually dealt and Marcia received – it was her choice to be largely passive in these instances. She waited, biting her bottom lip in anticipation.

Tavini had chosen to double-up for their sexual encounter that particular day. A small presentation microphone and an ivory letter opener were going to be his tools on this occasion. He had used the former implement on Levene before, but the sharp letter opener was making a first appearance.

The elegant forty-four year-old female had deliberately worn attire that accentuated her height and thin frame. Her black skirt, whilst fulfilling the requirements demanded by her front-line MC-Project status, had a long split down the left-hand side that made her sessions with David an easy form of indulgence to partake in.

As the ivory implement was teased down the contours of Levene's spine, Tavini utilised his other hand to guide the microphone between her vagina and anus. As his implement handling became more forceful, he uttered the type of language that fully activated Marcia's dark libido.

"Well, your sweat and pain are going to unlock the gates of Sodom today Ms Levene – that's if you can stay the pace!"

Marcia Levene rose to Tavini's challenge, arching her back to invite him in for anal penetration. Her riposte words made the man increase the force that he was using still further and the ivory implement started to leave some quite deep cuts on the woman's back. A small volume of blood started to evidence Tavini's

14

presence.

"Ever the charmer David! Are you going to carry on playing with those implements or do you intend to *properly* apply them!"

The woman's teasing choice of words prompted Tavini to bend her frame over the chair with an additional force that restricted the air entering her lungs. His left forearm encircled Marcia's windpipe, forcing her head upwards. In unison with this act, Tavini utilised his right elbow to apply downward blows to the small of Levene's back. The implements had been temporarily discarded, but after delivering a last vicious elbow-blow, Tavini reclaimed both of them to administer a fitting finale for their short violent encounter.

He proceeded to perform sodomy on the woman with the microphone and he inflicted *deeper* cuts with the letter opener between Levene's spinal vertebrae.

When the S&M show was over, Levene sank to her knees, her back bleeding and her rectum painfully pulsating. She smiled at David Tavini in a demure fashion, with grateful eyes. As she walked to her office wardrobe, she reached for her red suit – the camouflage to hide her blood. She turned to David and smiled in an innocent coy manner. She uttered two words in a gentle whisper.

"Thanks David."

*   *   *   *   *   *   *   *   *   *

Jess Wheeler climbed the four steps to the speaker's podium and greeted the protagonists behind the American Division of the MC-Project. His great height seemed accentuated still further as he stood on the small podium.

"I'm pleased to see you people. In the five years

15

since my predecessor finally stood down, I've seen our beloved project reach new heights surrounding the *control* of a potentially wayward First world populace.

"Our Prerogative Three modifications have been pivotal with regard to initiating a more passive global society. We always knew that if the negative drives lurking in the Auto-Vendetta sections of the brain were eradicated, a better, more controlled environment would ensue. I mean, when was our last riot? Sure we get isolated 'Avoider' skirmishes, but this kind of small-scale rebellion is basically like a breeze taking on a hurricane! We are that hurricane and anyone who opposes us will be nullified."

After a brief round of applause from most of those assembled Wheeler continued.

"I always felt that my predecessor Leif Dennison used to stand on ceremony too long at MC-Project meetings, a Vain-trait he could have done without – get it?

"Newer MC-staff wouldn't have got my in-joke just then, but I see acknowledgement in some of you old-hands! Sorry new-crew! That in-joke revolved around events twelve years back!

"Right I'll return to the Mr Wheeler that you've come to recognise and run our agenda by you.

"After my intro, Marcia Levene will detail the Avoider situation in Europe and the States. We will then be able to assess the latest Prerogative Three stats courtesy of Mr Sant and Professor David Tavini will volunteer the final input before we break into sub-sections. All yours Ms Levene."

Marcia approached the speaker's podium with confidence. The blood on her back was starting to solidify and as the woman faced the one hundred and fifty front-line personnel she was calm, with the inner peace that Sado-Masochism had brought her!

"I feel impelled to ensure everyone that the latest Avoider details are exactly as Mr Wheeler indicated. The Avoiders amount to nothing. They have few weapons, no base, no tactical edge and definitely no synergy or forward - planning. In short, the Avoiders are disparate types of nomadic scavengers."

Levene briefly drank some of the mineral water provided before she continued her address.

"In April 2005 one Avoider pack managed to destroy an MC-Project Designation structure in Seville. You will no doubt remember that isolated terrorist success, but that was some years back now and nothing of such devastation has transpired since.

"On that occasion we managed to catch all forty-three Avoiders and each was systematically executed on the charred site of the destroyed project base. These executions knocked the Avoiders back collectively and several groups turned themselves in for a Prerogative Three armistice. The European Avoider packs are now less in number and they are nearly always located in wilderness, several kilometres from urban areas.

"One small pack in England and another in a mountainous region of Germany occasionally manage to crack our epidermal infrastructure, but the odd blown bridge or derailed project train hardly amount to much in success terms. In all instances we are tightening the net on the Avoiders. They are easy to track from our surveillance planes and as they retreat further into the wilderness, they find fewer provisions to maintain their survival.

"We have performed 688 Main-Vault readings and over 400 mindsight readings on Avoider prisoners in the last decade and resistance patterns have emerged."

The crowd fixed Levene intently with their eyes,

because Avoider-pattern revelations would represent new material for their consumption. Until that point Avoiders had just been demeaned en-masse and Levene had commenced with that approach, but suddenly a word that implied configuration aroused curiosity in the ranks. Levene had detected the enhanced concentration and paused briefly before continuing.

"The Main-Vault revealed *heightened-visuals* that illuminated a vagrant existence, a *dog eat dog* culture where survival is firmly in the hands of a hierarchical structure.

"The Avoiders have leaders in each sub-group and a series of rules were evident in the majority of the pack members that we surveyed. The primary rule involves a no-breeding policy and this is closely aligned with the necessity to keep moving as far as their locale is concerned. These Main-Vault readings gave us images and sounds that kept reiterating my aforementioned Avoider criteria, but the Vault-Extension mindsight neurological-scans obviously delved into an individual's psyche to a deeper level and interesting results were found in this section of the brain. The Avoiders feel as you might expect them to – a quarry fleeing from us. Not surprisingly they exude a lot of hate, anger, aggression and yes, vendetta-spirit towards the MC-Project, but the vast majority of the individuals that we tested had stronger degrees of each negative emotion reserved for their own kind! We discovered that jealousy and envy pre-determined the thought patterns of most of our Avoider prisoners. We displayed on a laser screen the organisational chaos that breeds in the minds of each Avoider pack. Some of these packs will self-destruct before we get them and the minority that don't will be destroyed by the power of our MC-Project forces. Either way, the Avoiders are a doomed entity in this

world."

After her summary of the European Avoider situation, Levene spent two hours itemising the breakdown of Avoider groups across the United States. Her account was very detailed on a state-by-state basis and her words had a mesmerising effect on the American Division. She finished her Euro-American reconnaissance and waited for any questions that her colleagues may have had.

After a respectful silence MC-stalwart Blythe Carson spoke.

"You said that Avoider packs are easy to track via surveillance planes? With the military power that we have at our disposal, surely quick-fire eradication would be a formality? Doesn't the real reason behind Avoider retention involve curiosity on our part – to determine what exactly makes the Avoiders persevere in the face of such adversity? I ask you Ms Levene, do some of the highest rank and file believe that the Avoiders have retained a form of bonding that is antithetical to the rest of core-society? Do we *admire* them in part?"

Levene was momentarily taken aback by Carson's direct form of questioning. She cast a nervous glance at Wheeler, before she recovered her composure and then she continued in the attack-orientated riposte style that she had made her own.

"Perhaps you have been too long in the field Mr Carson. Many would argue that your words are tantamount to a form of project treason! In short, the Avoiders are our enemy and if you think that we hold them in admiration, I suggest that you enlist in the services of one of our very capable project-therapists. Yes we have the military prowess to take out 90% of the Euro-American Avoider groups, but the fiscal cost of such a mandate would run into billions.

"If the Avoiders were a homogenised military-machine, things would be different, but if you remember my previous words, you will realise that the Avoiders are merely disparate packs of scavengers playing out time.

"I have nothing against your initial question Mr Carson, but I objected to the word *admire* being utilised for the MC position regarding the Avoiders. Watch your language Blythe."

Levene then left the speaker's podium without giving Carson the chance to counter her reply. Mr Sant acknowledged her as she took her leave.

Marcia had been jolted by Carson's question. His words had disrupted what she felt had been a flawless performance up until that point. He had broken the ambiance that she had enjoyed and she hated him for daring to blemish her address. He was now a *marked* man in her eyes.

Marco Sant started to reveal the Prerogative Three statistics, now a decade in implementation, as far as First-world Auto-Vendetta eradications were concerned.

"A year ago, the United States of America were in pole position with regard to the implementation of Prerogative Three. We had terminated more Auto-Vendetta sections per-capita than any other First-world nation. Unfortunately we are now in second place."

The project ranks started to openly discuss Mr Sant's surprising announcement. America had always been the leading country for successful Prerogative Three *completions* until that point. Sant continued after Wheeler had *snarled* a call for silence.

"The Brits have secured an 83% completion rate. We are second with a 90% return, but our MC-Project friends in China can now boast an outstanding 93% figure.

"Other European countries closely follow Britain, but the big news obviously involves China turning in a performance that is up year-on-year. The Chinese have flown into the top-spot from nowhere! We now have to challenge for the optimum completion status for the first time. I have spoken about this rank change to Mr Wheeler and he feels that we will collectively learn from the transition. He has felt for some time that we were losing our sharpness in relation to Prerogative Three head-counts and the Chinese ascendancy obviously pays testimony to his suspicions.

"We are obviously determined to regain the highest rank in this control-based area and I know that Professor David Tavini is waiting to tell you about the Leanworld-Vision that his research team have formulated.

"*Leanworld* was a concept that was first devised seven years ago and it wasn't due for introduction for another decade, but Mr Wheeler is now keen to accelerate the implementation process. I will now let David guide you through the *Leanworld-Vision*."

Jess Wheeler deliberately hadn't divulged the subject matter that Tavini would relate to the MC ranks, because he wanted his project colleague to break the Vision in his racy verbal style and get straight to the point. In Wheeler's eyes, Tavini would be the slayer of the apathy that he felt had crept into sections of the American MC-Division. He knew that David's words would distress some of the cohort, but that is exactly what he wanted. Tavini's research area had been kept so secret that not even Levene had been privy to the development. Tavini always captivated his audience and his words on this occasion would prove to be his most significant revelation to date!

"Glad to see you MC-people. I'm glad to run the Leanworld-Vision by you.

"We waste too much time, too many dollars and too much energy on *nurse-maiding* those people who have been through Prerogative Three. What subsistence do you think our Chinese colleagues provide for their Prerogative Three graduates – nothing, zip-that's what! Their population is already down 16% on a year ago as a direct result of their no-provision decision. Leanworld means exactly what the syllables indicate – fewer people. This means no dependency with just the strong surviving.

"We aim to cut supply in three stages. In six months we will halve distribution and then after a year we will reduce provisions to 20% of the current level. The final stage will commence after a period of eighteen months and this stage will involve the removal of all food and liquid provisions. After this point the dependent masses won't slow us down anymore because most of them won't be around anymore! A much smaller First-world population will be in evidence and it will be elite-determined in nature. There will not be a need for Prerogative Three in this near-perfect state. You see we have to eradicate the cancer of the masses to let the cream realise their full potential. In effect we will be ushering in the fantasy of yesterday and making it our concrete tomorrow! Prerogative Three paves the way and the Leanworld-Vision realises our dream!"

"That's fucking *genocide* Tavini and you know it!"

Blythe Carson stood alone. His presence amidst the ranks of those silent seated around him, appeared as a very *singular* form of aberration. His confrontational words had been delivered from the heart and after years of challenging the MC party line he had come to expect support from some of his

colleagues. Several people did reiterate his feelings concerning the maltreatment of the masses in private, but none stood with him to be counted in opposition on this occasion. Carson felt that the Leanworld-Vision represented a new directive of tyrannical proportions and he had been convinced that the time to arrest the moral slide had been activated by Tavini's sick words. In a few seconds his expectation for solidarity had been crushed. Wheeler's menacing eyes and Tavini's manic ravings had silenced everyone but himself and he was left isolated in his defiance. The man continued with his attack nonetheless.

"Thanks for standing with me guys – where's your stomach for a fight gone? I guess that a mad Professor and the lynch-mob mentality that hangs over all of us, has finally forced you into submission! Don't you see how perfectly measured this whole fucking operation has been? Don't you realise that in this Leanworld bedlam there will be further sub-divisions of the favoured and then you could well become expendable.

"We have collectively soiled the First-World population in the last decade and now we are going to cast them free after neurologically destroying the survival-instincts that they would have possessed naturally. We control the media, we control security and we control state legislation, but one day our sins are going to be measured against us. Today my words will have set up my execution – we all know that. They may come quietly in the night, or a rogue project driver will mow me down, but we all know the score, we all know that this will be my *last farewell.* Wheeler, Tavini – I submit my resig-option now. You took great pleasure in giving staff that freedom five years ago didn't you? Well out of the few that took up the freedom-ticket, how many were seen again in the wider community? None! Not one fucking exception. They all disappeared, but unlike me they approached you privately with their resignation requests. At least I can say fuck the lot of you with some dignity left in my eyes!"

After his final project insult, Carson took his leave. He walked down the Assembly room aisle knowing full well that he was a dead man walking. He cast a final look back at the *ranks of the fearful* before taking the lift down to the outside world.

Upon reaching his MC-vehicle an idea came to him. It wasn't radical in its conception, but it gathered inspiration from his father's generation. He knew it had happened then, but protest had died in the New Age that he was a victim of.

The man unlocked the trunk of his vehicle and hauled out the fuel container. He proceeded to jog back up the sidewalk, stopping beneath an MC-Project building. Carson then ventured out into the middle of the litter-strewn highway and tipped the fuel on his High-Rank project clothing.

He sat cross-legged on the crumbling stone and scrawled a message on the surface of the highway. The man drank a small amount of fuel and then ignited himself. He was dead in seconds.

Carson was recovered later - a charred figure that still pointed an accusing finger up to the project building. His message had been untouched by the flames. It read as insult or inspiration depending on who would come across it...

...'*The Avoiders – Man's last Prayer.*'

TWO

The old man's trembling hand guided the coffee cup to his cracked lips and the gentle May sunshine provided a sharp contrast to the man's austere image. He sat huddled in his long overcoat, remembering the extremities of the recent cold winter. He hadn't been neurologically altered because they didn't fear an individual who approached his 103rd year. The gentleman sat alone at a table at an outside café in front of the *Hotel Kaiserworth*. He had been a resident of Goslar for the majority of his life and now he had been left to play out his existence in the realms of memory. The man had turned bitter after his friends had left him, either by the final journey or through the alterations performed upon them by the MC-Project.

The second group was usually younger in years and seemed as dead as those leaving in a coffin to all intents and purposes. They had returned to Goslar with a sickly, perpetual smile and their spirit had been drained from them. The man scowled as he pondered – there was more than one way to die. The provision lorry broke his train of thought when it arrived in the market-square. The mid-afternoon distribution of bread and water effectively marked time for the old man, if nothing else. Initially the handout had been quite exciting in it's novelty, but as the years progressed the people grew less distinguishable from each other in terms of behaviour and their totality lessened with each successive year.

The old man and the small crowd awaiting provisions weren't the only people who had witnessed the arrival of the vehicle. The binoculars of the Harz-based Avoiders had scanned the arrival from the lower slopes of the Harz Mountains. The word was given to advance via an acquired Comm-Lynx system and the pack sub-division on the outskirts of Goslar headed straight for the market-square.

The active group consisted of the seven most able street fighters. Their mission had a dual purpose, with a primary target that concerned the acquisition of food and liquid provisions. The secondary target involved the securing of any weapons from the MC-Project forces that were in attendance.

Taylor Wingate led the group; one of the British members of the Harz-pack and Feyer was second in command. She spoke fluent English, despite her Norwegian roots.

English was a linguistic common - denominator for the Harz-pack because most of the members were either British or American. The Scandinavian contingent was recruited when they resided in London as LSE students. After the MC-Project imposed closure on all educational centres eight years previous, the Avoiders had managed to rescue a few students before the vast majority were forced into a Prerogative Three modification programme.

Feyer had been one of the rescued. Ludmilla was the only Harz-pack Avoider who couldn't converse in English. Despite this setback, the thirty-one year-old Latvian had proved excellent in the field of survival and her skills had greatly assisted the other twenty-six pack members. In the three years that the pack had spent in the Harz Mountains, Ludmilla had saved the

lives of six of her fellow Avoiders.

The pack had enjoyed a period of ten months without suffering a fatality, but that particular afternoon would disrupt the new found equilibrium quite radically.

Feyer tightly clasped her Kalashnikov as the seven made their way into the market-square. The MC-Project driver was distributing the provisions to the assembled crowd, but he was oblivious to the advancing Avoiders as they approached him on his blindside. When the group were within a few metres of the distribution point, Wingate threw a knife at the man, with the precision of one who had seen Parachute Regiment active service.

The blade tore into the man's neck just below the jaw line and the shaft entered the back of the mouth. Despite the awesome placement of the throw, death wasn't instantaneous. The event was relatively silent because the man's vocal chords had been ripped out and as he thrashed on the ground he effectively drowned in a deluge of his own blood!

When the man fell to the ground, his provision sack landed amongst the waif-like throng. There was no recognition of the man's agony because the MC-Project had neurologically destroyed such comprehension and death was also an alien concept to people who only understood bliss.

For a brief moment the Avoiders were transfixed by the horror of encountering the *wasted* generation at such close proximity, but then they started to strip the vehicle of any items that their pack could utilise. Two of the group surveyed the market-square for any signs of additional MC-Project personnel, whilst the other five loaded their provision sacks. Everything was going to plan until a succession of bullets ripped into the face of Adam Redmond. He had been one of the two Avoiders watching over the square, but he hadn't anticipated that a crack project hit - squad was in placement on the second floor of the Hotel Kaiserworth.

When the Avoiders had raided Goslar eighteen months previous, old people or the wasted had occupied the square buildings. Usually the Avoiders didn't strike the same place twice and usually the Project didn't reserve a crack response squad should they break this singular pattern. On this occasion though both conventions had been aborted and Redmond's mutilated face was the first outcome surrounding the aberration of typical group practice.

Feyer had been in the lorry when Redmond had been killed, but she was the first to recover her composure and shout a tactical instruction to the rest.

"Spread the Full-Star guys. I'll see our neighbours."

The woman had conveyed a lot of detail into one short sentence and the group understood what must be done. The Full-Star reference meant that the pack must split in separate directions and Feyer had also indicated that she was in the best position to attack the hit - squad. Each Avoider had a memorised three-point compass direction by which they should scatter should a crisis situation materialise and being fired upon by an MC squad with a high-angle advantage definitely justified the calling of the crisis option!

When the Avoiders spread across the market – square in different directions, the hit – squad intensified their fire. They had a laser cannon in their possession in addition to the *favoured* Uzi and both types of weapon were now activated against the Harz – pack. The Project weapons cut through the ranks of the wasted Prerogative Three victims in a matter of seconds and the square was stained crimson with their blood.

A form of extermination was being carried out by the Project forces and some of the fleeing Avoiders stopped to return fire, believing that they stood a better chance of survival if they activated a response. Their *stand and fight* logic had been decided upon with carnage all around them and by abandoning the Full-Star they played into the hands of the enemy.

Panic had driven the four Avoiders to partake in the futile exchange of fire and as they hid behind rows of bloodied corpses, they became prime targets for the two American project staff that manned the laser cannon. The pair made light of their executions.

"No, leave *fat man* until the end Danny. Look at the slob cowering behind the bodies. Jeez, I thought the Avoiders were all skin and bone, but this guy's a fucking whale!"

It wasn't long before the laser cannon blasted three Avoiders and then the pair realigned the weapon on the individual who had inspired the cruel obesity remarks. They terrorised the poor man with the glee of schoolboys torturing insects.

"Yo, gotcha fucker! I blew his left leg off Macmillan, but the cunt is still sending it back! Jeez, he's bleeding like an evil Friday man! See what you can blow off him next buddy."

The pair had got so carried away with their sick commentary that they hadn't accounted for Feyer, or seen Wingate take evasive action down a narrow side street. The woman was their *primary* threat as she had managed to enter the ground floor of the hotel. Shortly after the exchange of fire began. She had slithered between the corpses of the provision victims and then she took refuge alongside the corpse of a frail old man. Then Feyer stealthily entered the hotel via the main entrance. There had been no one on the ground floor, no one to witness the arrival of a slight woman – reddened heavily by the blood of others.

She set to work quickly, anchoring steel traces to tactical points in the ground floor brickwork. When she was satisfied with her labyrinthine maze of fixing wire, she started to secure packs of plastic explosive at five key points. She perspired, she shook and her vaginal region hurt from the pain that she had inflicted there the previous day. Despite these barriers, Feyer remained resolute in her central purpose – to transform the Hotel Kaiserworth into a pile of ashes.

The laser cannon two floors above Feyer camouflaged any noise that she made and she was assisted further by the return – fire from the square. Eventually though both forms of weapon fell silent and the woman finished her task without making an audible sound. She then installed a crude clock – based detonation device. The Avoiders had acquired a limited amount of explosive material from their raids, but they hadn't come across any of the sonic detonators used by the Project. Feyer set the detonator for six minutes and then proceeded to quietly make her way to the hotel entrance. She knew that she had to head left once she was outside and so she crept across the fringes of the square. Shattered bodies lay all around her.

Feyer could discern low voices from the second floor and she heard the sound of triumphant laughter accompany the dialogue. Looking upwards over her left shoulder, she noted that three MC-Project hit-squad members were engaged in conversation. They were standing near an open second floor window, with their backs to the square. If one of them cast a downward glance to their right, Feyer would be noticed in an instant. As their congratulatory laughter increased in volume, Feyer heard a sound a few metres into the square. She couldn't immediately

detect whether it was a groan from the dying, or a pneumatic release from one of the melted corpses. When she did pinpoint where the sound came from, a shiver of horror ran through her frame.

Staring in her direction was Jack Clancy, one of her fellow Avoiders. His mangled body was a repugnant outcome of the laser cannon. Both his legs had been blasted away and his left arm was also absent. The man's right arm had been fused into his partially exposed rib cage and laser heat had melted the left hand side of his face.

Despite his appalling injuries, Clancy was still alive! He was in excruciating pain, but he wasn't dying through loss of blood because the laser had fused his limb endings. The man surveyed Feyer with his remaining eye. His request was pitiful as he spoke in a hoarse whisper.

"Finish me off Feyer. Take my head, so the bastards can't locate us. Please finish me."

The woman knew that Clancy was right. In the man's condition he was *beyond* help. She took a machete from her waist belt and proceeded across the corpses to where Jack Clancy was situated. His request to be decapitated made sense for all the Avoiders. He knew that unless this was done, the Project would read his Main MC-vault and illuminate the modus operandi and whereabouts of the Harz – pack.

As Feyer neared Clancy, she saw the bodies of other Avoiders and she realised that other heads would have to be taken. She said nothing to Clancy, but gave him a quick, kindly acknowledgement with her eyes, before severing his head with a single machete blow. She affixed the head to her belt, using the man's hair to secure a tight hold. Then Feyer set off further into the square to find another dead

Avoider.

As she neared the centre of the square she kept glancing up at the second floor of the Kaiserworth, in case one of the hit squad should look out and notice her. She had threaded her way through the bodies silently until she stumbled over a dead woman and fell heavily on her knees. The sound of the fall alerted her enemy immediately!

"Game on fellas – one's still alive! Blast the fucker Danny!"

"No chance man. They're a fucking *femme*. Look at her running! I'm just gonna wing the bitch and then we'll shag her brains out. We'll go two-up man and split her in half!

Feyer had started to sprint as soon as she realised that she had been spotted. As she approached the edge of the square she expected the laser cannon to blast her through the back, but she was felled by just one pistol bullet because her enemy had other plans for her flesh.

She had received a glancing bullet wound to her left cheek. As some blood flicked across her face, she momentarily lost consciousness. The woman was revived less than a minute later by two pairs of male hands pulling her clothing from her. They ripped off her jeans and one of her assailants then started to peel off his military uniform – whilst the other brandished an Uzi in her direction. He taunted Feyer as his partner undressed.

"Prepare yourself bitch. My buddy is a circumcised fucking stallion and just after he's rammed home, I'm gonna do you back-ways at the same fucking time!"

Feyer heard the sick words as blood rolled down her cheek, but she was focusing on her Kalashnikov. The gun was just a couple of metres behind her would-be rapists.

THE SCREAM OF FEYER

The undressing male had just discarded his trousers when the Hotel Kaiserworth blew apart. In a matter of seconds the hotel was reduced to a tangled mass of bricks and beams. Feyer only needed a second to realise her chance of escape. She felled the gun-toting individual with an upward kick to his testicles, whilst the explosion distracted him. Then the woman leapt for her gun and despatched her semi-naked attacker with a volley of shots to the base of his neck. She didn't have time to recover her jeans or worry about the location of other hit-squad personnel. Feyer knew that the explosion would bring a full project cohort to the area in a matter of minutes and so she fled barefoot from the scene of slaughter.

The woman tore through the back streets of Goslar in a state that reflected the savagery that she had encountered. Her facial wound dripped blood quite profusely; her limbs were covered in bruises and she was left wearing only her ripped shirt and ragged underwear. Her feet were severely battered by Goslar's cobbled streets and she fell on the hard surface three times. When Feyer encountered a shallow stream to run through on the outskirts of town, she was grateful for the pain-relief it generated and she managed to reach the lower slopes of the Harz mountains after quite a short duration.

When Feyer was a couple of kilometres from the valley where the Harz-pack were temporarily based, she heard the distinctive drone of a project helicopter and she instinctively reached for her supply-bag. Her heart sank when she realised that the bag had been left in Goslar. The helicopter had the most advanced heat-seeking detection equipment and Feyer knew that it was capable of pinpointing humans in the deepest foliage. She had seen two of her fellow Avoiders killed by a seek and destroy chopper in the past.

The Harz-pack had acquired a masking spray for heat sensitivity in one of their raids on a ruined military base two years previous, but her canister was one of the essential items that her bag had contained. As the drone of the chopper grew louder Feyer didn't panic, but remembered alternative masking agents that Ludmilla had shown her. Although the Latvian communicated largely by gesture she had openly laughed at the masking spray when the pack leaders exhibited the canisters and in private she had shown Feyer a natural ingredient that fulfilled the same function. The exchange had been quite surreal without language. Ludmilla had smeared herself with a brown substance that she had located in the soil beneath one of the types of fir-tree that abounded on the lower slopes. When the woman had smeared her entire body, she had made a shallow trench in the soft woodland floor and then she had pulled undergrowth on top of her. After her demonstration, she pointed to the sky and signed the whirling rota-blades of a helicopter. Then Ludmilla had pointed to her smeared body and had signed a cross to imply that the chopper couldn't find her. That demonstration from the Latvian had been the first real communication between the pair and although her command of English was still very minimal, she and Feyer had become close pack members through signing as the years unfolded.

Feyer quickly located the correct type of fir-tree and proceeded to scrape brown sediment and lichen from the earth around the trunk. Once she had accumulated her *paint*, she shed all her remaining clothes in a matter of seconds. She started to daub the substance all over her body and in order to cover her back; she lay down and pressed her spine firmly into the camouflage. She writhed left and then right in

order to fully cover herself. The woman didn't have time to scrape a trench because the helicopter was almost directly over the small thicket that she was hiding in. She pulled a pile of leaves over her frame and rested her head on her sodden clothing. Finally she applied handfuls of moistened sediment to the facial bullet wound and her vagina because she didn't want blood illuminating her presence. The heat-seeking equipment would be activated fully by human blood.

The chopper passed over Feyer's position very quickly, but then it circled around the surrounding airspace for twenty minutes. Just when Feyer thought that the chopper was heading away it came back! On this occasion the surveillance involved the craft travelling at a greatly reduced speed at a height of no more than thirty metres. It would hover in a fixed spot at random intervals and the woman was petrified that her leaf-based camouflage would be blown from her due to the down-wind that the helicopter generated. A cold sweat broke out on the woman's body and this added to her fears of detection. She could do nothing about this physical excretion though and as the chopper drew even nearer she fainted through nervous exhaustion.

When Feyer eventually came to, darkness had fallen. She was completely naked, cold and thankfully – alone.

The chopper must have passed very close to her position, because all the foliage that she had pulled on top of her was scattered a few metres away. The woman left the daubing materials on her body and after pulling on her clothes; she started to search for her gun. Feyer had thought that she had hidden the Kalashnikov close by, but her search proved fruitless in the darkness and she had to give the weapon up as

35

a lost cause. As she neared the region where the Avoiders were based she fell heavily on the rough terrain, but managed to drag her battered body onwards. Her tenacious spirit became her guide.

The Avoiders had found a temporary cave-base in the Harz foothills and on that particular night the chosen pair of sentries were Dean Blackwell and Ludmilla. When the pair shone their torches on the approaching Feyer, recognition took them some time. It was only when she stumbled forward that Blackwell recognised the savage eyes that typified Feyer. He managed to arrest her fall and help her into the cave. As Avoider eyes scanned her entrance, Dean saw that she was overcome with her journey. He asked one question to her before Ludmilla could dress her wounds.

"Hey *painted* lady where the hell did you get to."

Feyer's reply summed up the extremities of her day.

"To the land of *rapists and zombies* Blackwell – get my message?"

THree

Feyer spent thirty-six hours recovering from the horrors of Goslar. She had slept for the best part of a day and then a medically trained Avoider, Dr Robertson had treated Feyer's wounds.

Her glancing bullet wound had been cleaned out thoroughly and a dozen stitches held her skin together. Her feet had been severely bruised and both had been bandaged quite tightly. Robertson had treated Feyer's vagina with the utmost professionalism given the fact that the Avoiders were without any implements to properly address internal bleeding. He hadn't asked the woman any awkward questions, but his eyes had shown curiosity on occasions. Feyer thought that he probably recognised the self-inflicted nature of the injury, but if that was the case - he said nothing. The woman had been given an old pair of crutches to move about on and as she tested them for mobility, Blackwell entered her section of the cave. His tone was sympathetic – even caring.

"Hi Feyer. Great to see you again. I guess that was some fucking ordeal! Only you and Wingate made it back, you know. Still, if fate only allowed a couple of survivors, I'm bloody glad you were one of them. You've been the talk of the pack whilst you slept.

Wingate thought that you might have got the *heads*. He didn't say he'd been knocked out by a laser cannon blast!"

Feyer digested Blackwell's words for a few seconds before delivering a *choice* response.

"After Redmond was wasted I called for a Full-Star retreat - but all hell broke loose when our guys stopped to return fire. The laser cannon crew took out everyone apart from Wingate and myself. Clancy was one of those fried by the laser and I performed a *Decap* on him, tying his head to my belt. I was trying to get the other heads, when I tripped over a corpse in the square and the bastards spotted me in seconds. I was brought down by a glancing shot because the fuckers wanted to double-rape me, but then the Kaiserworth blew and I took full advantage of the distraction! I lost just about everything during my escape including Clancy's head! In short, the project have got five Avoider minds to read. I didn't realise Wingate made it because I lost sight of him after Redmond was wiped out."

The pair continued to discuss Feyer's escape for some time and the woman knew that the infatuation Blackwell had for her, would be a far cry from the severity that she would receive from Michael Anderson – the leader of the Avoiders. Anderson had called an afternoon assembly for the whole pack in a copse that was close to the caves. Feyer expected verbal castigation from Anderson, but as she made her way to the assembly on her crutches, she became determined not to become Wingate's patsy.

The Avoiders stood in a circle to undertake the assembly, but Feyer was permitted to lean against a broad oak tree due to her condition. Anderson launched into a heated polemic at the start of the assembly.

"The provisions raid on Goslar was an

unmitigated disaster. Let me qualify this statement for everyone. Five Avoiders were killed and yet no heads were recovered. No provisions were acquired with regard to food stocks and weapons. One further supply pack was lost and one Kalashnikov was mislaid. The Avoider who was second-in-command during the raid received injuries that will restrict her mobility for a week or more. What the hell went wrong in Goslar we ask ourselves! Our reconnaissance binoculars only noted a small number of MC-Project personnel commanding a laser cannon and therefore we have to ask ourselves one burning question. Why did our crack troops scatter when faced with such a paltry resistance force?"

Anderson let the Avoiders verbally review the Goslar raid with each other before he continued.

"We have left too much pack evidence in Goslar. Each dead-head will be examined by the MC-Project and the brains of the dead will reveal thousands of images that will effectively lay us open! They will see our chain of command, probe our survival mechanisms and expose the criteria that shape our temporary mountain base. Some of our dead colleagues may well have received brain injuries that have left them unsuitable for neurological examination, but they only need one mind with an intact Main-Vault section to do us untold damage. Whilst we have never been a pack that has never favoured the maximum disciplinary penalty, I feel in this particular instance that both Mr Wingate and Feyer should account for this very dangerous failure."

Taylor Wingate was summoned to the centre of the circle and Feyer wondered what his *order of events* would be. She hadn't seen him rendered unconscious by the laser blast and wondered if he hadn't run out on the rest of the provisions group. She hadn't any firm evidence to back up this suspicion, just Wingate's gaze avoidance when she looked in his direction. Anderson began his questioning.

"Five out of seven dead is a painful fact to swallow Taylor. What the hell happened down in Goslar?"

Wingate ran the events by the group as they had happened in actuality, until Redmond's death. Then he switched from the real and began an account of pure falsehood.

"Once I realised that Redmond was beyond help, I started to return fire towards the *third* floor of the Kaiserworth with the other guys. We were doing well until Feyer called for a Full-Star retreat, and then the men were cut down by the laser cannon. A shot from that weapon eventually came in my vicinity and the blast knocked me out for some minutes. When I regained consciousness, Feyer was absent and all the others were dead. I was going to retrieve the heads of our crew, but then I came under fire and made for the back streets. My Kalashnikov had jammed and this factor forced my retreat. I kept calling for Feyer, but I think in hindsight that she had fled the scene. I could only hope that she was in hiding and would gather the heads if the gun-crew chased after me. Obviously my hopes were dashed when the woman returned with nothing, save *half* her clothing."

Wingate's *pack of lies* inflamed the anger building up inside Feyer. The *questioning* nature of his final falsehood was her breaking point and she launched into a scathing attack on the man who she now saw on a par with the scum she had left behind in Goslar.

"Fuck you Wingate, you callous lying bastard! I didn't even see you fire your gun!

"I called for the Full-Star when Redmond was killed not *after* the others returned fire. You just spouted a stream of bullshit there! Why don't you come clean and describe things as they actually

happened?"

The woman's initial outburst hadn't yet proved cathartic and as his words kept replaying in her mind, she became even more incensed.

"You think I *fled the scene* do you fucker? No one gets away with that type of slur on me! You aren't going to get away with inferring things about me to the pack you bastard! Yes I returned with *half* my clothing as you damned well emphasised, but everyone saw your suggestive look when you said that line. Get off over a woman's clothing do you, you sleazy bastard? Well I'm going to ram this ragged shirt down your fucking throat! I'm-"

Anderson had let Feyer boil up with anger, but now he felt an interruption was needed.

"Hey let's cool things down Feyer. Take a look at yourself woman! What do you aim to do exactly – drop one of our toughest Avoiders with one of your crutches?"

"I don't give a fuck. I was nearly raped in that mortuary down there and he says that I was fucking hiding!"

"We *know* you weren't Feyer."

"What do you mean *know*? You wouldn't have been able to see the details of what actually took place in the market-square from up here. I can see how you could have spotted the second-floor laser cannon crew but you couldn't have seen the massacre in the square in detail?"

She had glared at Wingate when she had correctly detailed the laser cannon location and then the certainty in Anderson's voice started to penetrate. As Feyer briefly fell silent, Anderson decided that it was time to drop his bombshell.

"We were *there* Feyer. Luke Bridges saw everything from the fringes of the square. He was our *shadow.* Luke has always shadowed active provision squads. He reports directly to me and until Goslar, it was good news after good news. None of the pack knew about shadowing until now – there was no need to illuminate this form of surveillance. His role has always involved assessing the method of operation. He follows provision squads in and gets out when the raid is nearly completed – or as in the case of Goslar, when the specific aims of the squad are thwarted."

Feyer's anger returned.

"So that *toad* leaves when the shit hits the fan does he? Before I'm going to get gangbanged by a couple of project perverts!"

"Yes, but not before he's seen your supposed leader scuttle away when the gunfight kicked off, or before witnessing you setting the charges that blew the Kaiserworth. He left after the last of the five died; they had ignored the correct order that you gave them. Do you see why our shadows have a use now Feyer? Do you see how they can tell me the truth Mr Wingate?"

Feyer was stunned and her emotions were quite confused. Her anger had initially increased when she felt that someone could have eased the pain she went through in Goslar, but she also felt a sense of jubilation because the whole pack had heard her words validated by their leader – exposing Wingate as a liar at the same time.

Anderson spoke again.

"Sorry for letting you suffer Mr Wingate's lies Feyer, but we had to let the truth be established in front of the whole pack, after the failure in Goslar, you became their collective Saint, but Mr Wingate didn't catch your spirit did he? Instead he has become the incarnation of cowardice – with treachery thrown in for good measure. Unfortunately your disgusting behaviour has forced my next move Taylor."

Anderson quickly drew his pistol, fitted the silencer and pointed it at the astonished unarmed pack member. Wingate didn't have time to plead for clemency as a bullet ripped through his main neurological vault! Anderson realised that his new hard line approach had shocked the Avoiders and a uniform silence hung over the execution venue for some thirty seconds after the killing. He then closed the assembly with orders that encapsulated his new authoritarian form of control.

"We are going to leave this base tonight and find another temporary base deeper into the mountains. The project is going to know about this base when they scan the *dead-heads* and we aren't going to wait around to be massacred. Feyer will follow the rest of us in three days time, once her injuries have recovered slightly. She can hand pick three Avoiders to remain with her and I will detail our rough location to her, before our departure. This assembly is now closed."

The pack made their way back to the caves, reflecting on the change that had come over Anderson. He had felled Wingate in a single act of calculated brutality. Some Avoiders privately felt that his *summary-execution* bore the hallmarks of MC-Project discipline and not the democratic style of leadership that they had become accustomed to. Even Feyer had been disturbed by the finality of Anderson's discipline. She had hated Wingate twenty minutes earlier, when he tried to transfer his cowardice to herself, but despite this factor she couldn't justify the execution of a man who had previously been a very dedicated pack member.

Later Anderson gave Feyer some written coded details surrounding the pack's next Harz base and he instructed the woman to select the sentinels who would remain with her whilst she recovered.

Feyer asked Ludmilla, Blackwell and another British Avoider called Matthew Reed to remain with her. None of the three expressed any objection to her request and they inwardly felt very honoured by their selection.

Feyer hated resting as the others took turns in looking out for project forces and by the middle of the third day she couldn't stand her incarceration any longer. The woman ripped off her bandages and started to partake in the rigorous training schedule that she had become accustomed to. As she shadow - boxed in the candlelit cave interior, sweat glistened on her brow. Her lithe frame may have been quite elfin on a first sighting, but the woman possessed a power that belied her slight exterior. She had rightly acquired a position of high rank in the Harz – pack through both physical strength and her astute leadership qualities. After finishing her exercises, she left the cave and located her three pack colleagues. She had decided to take a radical initiative and her group were going to be offered their own unique agenda. She spoke in a concise style of language that got straight to the point.

"I'm not going deeper into the mountains folks. That move plays into the hands of the MC-Project. Anderson may feel that his new *get tough* attitude will keep the pack together, but I don't want to be part of a system of control that breaks the solidarity of the past. When the *dead-heads* reveal their visual story, the project will apply form to the Harz – pack and they will see that we have implemented a higher-up deeper-in base transfer time after time. When have we ever *returned* to a place where the project ran us ragged? *Never* is the word you are looking for."

Matthew Reed spoke out against Feyer's line of argument.

"Return to Goslar Feyer? We'd be cut to pieces if

we went back there! Five Avoiders were wiped out in that fucking place and you were nearly raped. How the hell can you contemplate returning to that scene of carnage?"

"Easily Matt! Think about it. The last place the project would expect us to relocate would be Goslar. It's only a matter of time before they locate Anderson and the others. Our small group would just be lambs to the slaughter-if we follow their lead. Don't you understand folks – the freedom party's over! They've got too much on us now. We need to fragment the pack because some of us just might sink back into hiding if we scatter from the main pack. If our small pack initiated this splinter-logic, the whole pack would eventually catch our spirit and break away in small groups – if they survive that long that is! You three can do what you want though and anyone who wants to rejoin the others can have the relocation details that Anderson left me. I'm going back to Goslar tonight. An empty house won't be hard to find in a town of the dead and dying!

"During the day I'll feign vagrant identity until I can find a long – term venue to escape those bastards. Don't you see the best hiding place is in the jaws of our enemy! I'll give you five minutes to discuss where you want to go."

Ludmilla and Blackwell didn't need time to look at the options and they stood by Feyer, united in their support for her. When he realised that one was now three, Matt Reed followed suit. His words lacked the certainty of the gestures of the other two.

"I guess you're right Feyer. I can't help feeling that we're running out on the others though."

When the four of them reached the fringes of Goslar late that evening, eight fighter planes screamed high over their heads and then the distant mountain range was briefly lit up with tracer fire. No one said anything but everyone knew.

four

The form writhed in the icy depths and darkness enveloped its frame. Splinters of blue ice tore into *Klue's* lungs, but as the surface drew nearer the creature's savage rejuvenation began. The eyes bore through the blackness as the strength of the predator grew. Moonlight started to penetrate down through the Lofoten waters and this furthered the dark inspiration that pushed the creature upwards. Klue sensed the imminence of the second arrival and fetid excretions were expelled from the form as the moment approached.

With only seconds left. The propulsion turned the creature momentarily on its side, but a vertical entry position was regained by wild thrashing strokes from the hind - quarters. The beast tore into the world for a second time, amidst a cloak of Phosphorescence and Klue was catapulted a few metres above the surface – due to the cumulative pressure behind the upward journey.

As it trod water, saliva was brushed from the mouth: like a man in motion but essentially a creature through the frame. It sensed land and moved towards the indistinct mass close by. It sensed prey but wanted to tame the misery of hunger - lock it in place

with cruel desires that allowed play before the kill. Klue trembled as a hunter's anticipation coursed through cold veins. It had been too long, so he was going to savour the first slaying – starve himself just that bit longer until they arrived on the scene. He expected them, the unwitting servants of his black desires – the sacrifice to usher in his rebirth.

As his form contacted land, he drew himself up to his full height. Klue was a man when he needed that shape, but a beast when he revealed his true nature.

Both forms entwined as he surveyed the Maelstrom. He waited for them, his glinting eyes forcing a cold marriage with the dark waters. They would come.

*   *   *   *   *

Klue slept on a hard rock until the light of dawn awakened him. His eyes instantly returned to the sea and a small fishing vessel could be seen navigating the channel. The Maelstrom was Klue's playground and the four fishermen were about to receive his blessing for the first and last time.

The beast climbed higher up the outcrop and hatefully stared at his liquid domain. A faint smile creased his face as the first ripples of his presence spread across the water. Klue flexed his lean frame and let his malevolence incite the Maelstrom. As the waves increased in height the fishermen looked upwards to the darkening sky. The skipper feared the vortex that had claimed the lives of so many that had tried to navigate these harsh waters. He gave the order to return to port, but then Klue started to spin the currents, forcing the vessel into the circular movement that signified an impending whirlpool. A white sea mist blew across the channel and the waves rose to an awesome sight. The vessel had now been sucked into the eye of the Maelstrom and Klue directed the impending tragedy from his dark pulpit.

As the waves increased in force a howling wind could be heard, but the screams of those on the boat still managed to penetrate the chaos. Klue smiled as he heard them suffer. He enjoyed prolonging the torture of his victims and when the waves looked like they would suck the vessel under, he would relax his hold just a little, let the boat spin out to a calmer area and raise the hopes of the four men on board. After the bluff the creature would pull the vessel back into the whirlpool and the screams would rise again. Klue tired of playing after his sixth mock – release and he sank the boat with a savage fell swoop. As the boat was pulled deeper down it split apart and the four occupants drowned before their lungs exploded with the pressure. Their dead faces told the story of Klue's torture, but none would see the portraits of suffering because both the wreckage and corpses sank into the oblivion of the darkest fathoms.

After his work was done, Klue lay outstretched on the stark rock outcrop. His chameleon form melted into his surroundings. He had enjoyed his play, but he looked forward to the impending days when his enemy would seek him out. A journey would call him soon, but on that morning he was savouring his rebirth. This was his lair and his Lofoten outpost had a fitting name to carry his presence. The Lofoten people knew his temporary home by a memorable name – Hell!

five

Water dripped into the cellar of the dilapidated Goslar residence. The floors above Feyer's pack weren't inhabited, but project searchlights often penetrated the upper stories after darkness fell. It was this factor that forced the four Avoiders to share their nightlife with black rats in the recesses of the cellar. During the day everyone except Feyer, wore rags and mimicked the wasted expressions of the Prerogative Three victims around them. They queued for provisions like the others and managed to steal tinned foods from abandoned shops. Feyer couldn't go with the rest for fear of being recognised by MC-Project sources and thus her incarceration had been total. The pack had spent a week in the cellar and the woman was becoming stir – crazy!

On the eighth evening Feyer actually managed to go into a deep sleep. Usually the damp and the rats would wake her several times during the night, but on this occasion she was dead to the world. Blackwell was on sentry duty that evening and he had stolen a couple of furtive glances at his dark haired leader as she lay sleeping. He adored the woman, but they had only been intimate once a couple of months back and now her eyes had a keep away look about them. He hoped that one day she would lighten up again, but right now he felt that there was too much fire in her mind.

As Feyer entered R.E.M her mindsight started flooding her brain with an assortment of disparate images. Recollections of Wingate and Anderson intertwined with juvenile recollections from her childhood days in Norway. The deep sleep kaleidoscope suddenly started to fade, diminishing into a blanket of darkness.

A series of non-activated images then forced their way into the woman's mind. Feyer looked down on a moonlit sea from a viewing position high in the clouds. She enjoyed the space of a bird, although no species was registered and she would experience a feeling of plummeting descent before rising again to her previous high altitude. A faint smile emanated from the corners of Feyer's mouth, because she was essentially enjoying her metaphysical gliding at this stage. Something broke the surface of the sea below her and immediately the woman dropped to survey what had entered her dream world.

As she dropped nearer to the source that had risen from beneath the waves, a fetid scent rose upwards to check her descent. Whilst the woman had seen through the darkness with the clarity of a night bird, the foul stench activated a very human revulsion in the dreamer. She was experiencing a surreal state where the visionary was anchored by the real.

Blackness temporarily interrupted the images, as the woman twisted uneasily in her sleep. When she settled, the images returned and it was daylight. She had a ground – level perspective now and she observed a craggy rock outcrop nearby. She overlooked a cold sea and a mist was thickening over her vista. The putrid smell was now far more pungent and the human side of the dreamer felt bile rise in her throat. Something arose right in front of her, but it faced the sea and she couldn't discern the face of the

creature. She noticed the black plated texture of the
form in front of her, but then panic overcharged her
system and the dreamer once again took flight.

Feyer experienced a horizontal trajectory when she
left the outcrop and she viewed her surroundings at
great speed – just a couple of metres above the now
turbulent waves. As she started to rise, she saw a
small boat caught up in a violent whirlpool. Her
vision wouldn't release her upwards though and she
was forced to witness the suffering of the boat's
occupants time after time. The screams of those on
board pierced the woman's psyche, leaving an
indelible register. When the vessel eventually broke
apart the dreamer was forced under the waves, seeing
death at touching – distance. The dying still released
screams that penetrated to Feyer through the depths
and her last recollection of the vision involved life
draining from one of the victims. His eyes rolled
white and his face was like a pallid death – mask
sinking deeper in the water.

"Feyer! Yo Feyer! Come round now. Wake up for
fucks sake! Please woman wake up!"

The voice belonged to Blackwell. Feyer had been
thrashing from side to side and knocking her body
against the hard cellar walls. It had taken the efforts
of all three Avoiders to restrain her and yet even when
she regained full consciousness, it took her a few
minutes to regain full cognisance of her surroundings.
Feyer had vomit over her clothing and scratches were
apparent on her arms. When she had recovered a little
Blackwell spoke again.

"Jeez Feyer! You were like a woman possessed
then. What the hell were you dreaming about?"

"It was like some virtual-death program. I can't
make any sense of it. The images were mainly based
on memories I guess, but I can't account for some

bits! I just don't fucking know!"

She then turned on her side and retched again as the fetid smell returned to her nostrils.

Thousands of kilometres away in Washington, Jess Wheeler kicked over his desk in frustration. He was alone, examining the laser footage of recent MC-Vault explorations and his private agenda wasn't being realised. It had been over twelve years since he had first learnt that the Main MC-Vault may hold answers to some of man's eternal questions and Wheeler had been the executioner of the person that carried out this private research. For the last four years, he like Mr Fray before him, had been fascinated by the opportunity to prove the existence of gods or devils. When he achieved Project – Leader status, he had ensured that one security unit had a sole duty that was concerned with the acquisition of individuals that professed to have seen God or were reputed to be possessed. Each individual had been placed in cryogenic storage, until they could be made ready for exploration.

When one of the selected was reanimated, Wheeler would instruct his team to perform visual operations on the Main MC-Vault and the vault-extension in some cases.

After the explorations had been undertaken, he would activate a laser screen and review the mental imagery. When he commenced his surveillance, he felt confident that he would discover conclusive visual footage that proved the existence of a more powerful being or presence.

After four years undertaking his self-appointed quest, his enthusiasm had dulled. On occasions indistinct shapes or coloured masses had promised great things, but these visuals had been supported by muffled sounds as opposed to any recognisable

language. He had just finished his latest trawl and once again nothing significant had materialised. Wheeler turned off his laser screen and put his desk back in an upright position. He was located in an underground research section of a project base and the place had an oppressive feel about it. He glanced at the clock and saw that it was 10:06pm. The man had been undertaking his research for a seven-hour stretch that day and his mouth was parched. He headed for the door looking forward to a refreshing drink. Before he reached the door, the strip lighting flickered then died. A voice cut through the darkness and Jess Wheeler shivered. The tone was deep and yet the utterance had a pitch that fluctuated in volume – almost as if the source was continually shifting their position.

"Looking for me Je*ss*?"

Wheeler had been unnerved by the speaker's decision to hiss the last two letters of his name and he moved towards the door area tentatively. He gave the speaker an angry reply.

"Some fucking joke! If you are pissing around with an *effects* microphone Tavini, I'll break you Mr America!"

A pregnant silence pervaded the room. Wheeler had waited for a humorous riposte, but something inside him knew that one wouldn't be forthcoming. The laser screen emitted a faint green glow after being shut down and his eyes started to partially discern the layout of his research quarters, He became aware of a presence adjacent to his stacked filing cabinets. For the first time in his life, Jess Wheeler felt acute fear, because he began to deduce the size of whoever was in the room with him. The cabinets were two metres in height, but the occupant standing next to them was much taller! Another voice came from the now stationary form – the far away whine of a young girl. Every word echoed...

"So cold Mister, so lost. I need friend. You my friend?"

"What the fuck are you?"

The child's voice came back.

"We serve Klue. I serve Klue. I *am* Klue."

"Who the hell is Klue?"

"Klue lives in Hell. You know that – you *called* him."

Wheeler started to lose his temper, becoming angered by the echoing childish whine. His next response was subsequently more savage than his previous utterances.

"Look, get me the main man back kid. Where the fuck are you hiding anyway?"

The MC-Project Leader was literally knocked from his feet as the malevolent deep voice returned. He was about to meet what he had tried so hard to find.

"She's in *me* fucker. We are one of the same. Everyone feeds my frame if I choose it. Your fucking mother Jess, your fucking kids, your whore of a wife if I allow her. The whole rotting world comes through me and dies in me. Their sorrow is my salvation. You just fell Jess. I thought your fall - I conceived it. In a few seconds I'm going to break some of your bones Jess. I'll break them without touching. I'll think break and the chosen bones will fucking snap. You invited me Wheeler. I am Klue, the frozen river, the famine landscape. I am the voice of pestilence and in the beautifully sick world you've created, I am a natural product. I'm going to think about you Jess!"

The silence returned to the room and Wheeler cowered on the floor, wondering which bones Klue would break. A warm heat started to pulse around his body and when the heat intensified around his ribs, Klue made his first break. The rib snapped like a

twig, but Wheeler had lost the power to scream. He shook with fear as the heat started to travel through him again. As the heat started to intensify around Wheeler's groin area, the girl's voice returned to the room of darkness.

"*There* Father - Hurt him *there*!"

Klue contemplated what his twisted juvenile side had instructed him to do. He held the Project Leader in a state of fearful anticipation without saying a word. As the intense heat localised great pressure over Wheeler's genital area, the victim lost control and urinated in his clothing. He was experiencing the type of extreme terror that he had inflicted on countless others during his MC-Project years and a bizarre kind of equalisation was taking place. The dominant side to Klue spoke again.

"Are you glad that you found me Jess? Suffering is my art you know! You can't see me yet Mr Wheeler, but at least you are gently experiencing my presence. Another part of me wants to *destroy* an area of your body that you may wish to retain, but I think she has left the room. Do you want me to invite her back or shall I choose another area to *ruin*?'

Wheeler sobbed like a child and started to plead for clemency.

"Please spare me Klue. Please, please stop the torture. I beg you to leave me intact. You can have anything, anyone!"

"I know I can. What the fuck can *you* give me?"

A familiar voice interrupted.

"Nothing Father. He can't give you anything. Put him through a *slow* kill."

"Leave me child. I have a role for Wheeler. You hear that Jess. Yes I can use you. You need to vomit don't you – so be it."

Jess Wheeler's whole frame went into seizure as he

retched for a few minutes. After the bile came, the blood and when it was done, exhaustion came over him. He recovered some hours later and sensed that he was alone in the darkness. His broken rib hurt him, but he struggled to his feet as the room lights flickered back on.

Devastation met his eyes. A fetid smell hung over the cabinet area and the floor was partially covered in blood, vomit and urine. His exploration equipment had been ruined by something and shards of ice splinters were impaled in functional objects throughout the room. Wheeler trembled when he remembered Klue's parting words. For him, it looked as though survival depended on staying in league with the devil!

six

Jess Wheeler didn't divulge any information about Klue to his project subordinates. Although as leader, he was free to do as he pleased, he didn't want too many people to learn of the specifics behind his hidden agenda work. David Tavini had noticed that Wheeler winced with pain on occasions and frequently held his mid-rift, but when he asked if his leader was in ill health, he had received a very curt negative. Wheeler conducted his project business as usual, but he felt like the walking dead in many respects because he knew that Klue would be back. Jess knew that Klue had a role for him, but he also anticipated that pain would be the hallmark of his duties.

The unenlightened ranks of the other MC-Project *elite* continued with their decadent power-obsessed lifestyles. No one exceeded the parameters of debauchery better than Marcia Levene. She used her high rank to give her a hedonistic buzz on a daily basis. She was addicted to libido enhancing performance drugs and one of her favourite leisure pursuits was known as *Necsexing*. This was a practice enjoyed by those who retained intellectual control and it involved the elite driving through the ghettos that housed Prerogative Three victims to select individuals who would be used as tools for their sexual gratification.

Once the elite individual or group had finished with their victim, they would shoot them and append a branding tag to the body. The tag was a barbed metal construction that would stay on the body until it decomposed. The name of the tagger was displayed on the metal.

Necsexing had been in vogue for close on a decade now and Levene never tired of this vicious pursuit. She preferred to hunt in a *duo* and on the morning after Wheeler's satanic visitation, she was hunting with a non-project girlfriend called Saskia Rivette.

Levene drove her convertible at high speed to the favoured Ghetto 7. Saskia sat beside her, in a very short skirt that fully exposed her prime reason for visiting the ghetto. She didn't have any briefs on and began to sexually moisten herself, as the car got closer. Her careless black hair blew back to its full extent and the pair laughed wildly when they reached their intended destination.

Levene got out first and as Saskia began to climb out of the vehicle, she was roughly forced back into her seat. Levene rammed her tongue deep into the woman's mouth before pausing to speak.

"Cool Sas! Name our prey – Stags or Does?"

"Stags in the ghetto Marce. We can always go doe to doe later."

"OK, but here's a taster first."

With that line, Levene raised Saskia's legs above her head and proceeded to perform oral sex on her. As her tongue probed deeper the woman started to dig her nails into the leather of the car seat. Marcia inserted two digits into her partner's vagina and when these were combined with her pointed tongue, Saskia came in a matter of seconds. The seat glistened with the woman's juices.

After Levene serviced Saskia, the pair made their

way to the Ghetto 7 compound. They both clutched their *branding* tags and laughed when they saw the first group of tagged corpses nearby. The women put on facial masks to counteract the stench of the decomposing flesh around them and then they started to determine the identities of those who had beaten them to this particular patch. The pair didn't recognise some of the names, but Marcia suddenly located the name of a person who worked for the MC-Project with her. In an excited yell she asked Saskia to come and examine the tag.

"Yo Sas – jackpot! This guy's one of us! Marco Sant is a big player. I didn't know that the fucker *Necsexed.* Wait until I see him tomorrow!"

"I can't even tell if this *stiff* is a *Stag* or a *Doe* Marce. Does he play things straight or *Seed-Drill* both genders like us?"

"He's straight I think Sas. I don't really know Sant that well, but its kind of strange to find a tagger from project ranks in our stalking ground. Part of me is hyper fucked off, because this is our special turf – our private *sperm-bank.*"

After the woman had scanned the tags on some of the other rotting corpses, they made their way into one of the crumbling tower blocks that typified Ghetto 7. Soon they encountered the ranks of the wasted Prerogative Three victims, congregating in groups on the stairs between floors. When Levene and Rivette were sighted they were met with the familiar *diminished* smiles of the MC-Project victims. As they climbed higher up the structure, they found fewer corpses. Rivette commented on this factor on floor four and Levene told her that the floor above held the answer. She had been to Ghetto 7 countless times before, whereas her twenty-eight year old bi-sexual partner was making only her second visit.

Floor five held a macabre surprise for Rivette. When she reached the top of the stairs Levene beckoned her to come and look down the open lift shaft. The woman duly peered down and was shocked to see a pile of rotting corpses less than three metres below her. Marcia shed some light on the grisly discovery.

"They're compressed all the way down to the ground floor Sas. Throwing the corpses down the shaft has become a fucking *game* for the wasted. They haven't any concept of death as you know and so packing the *stiffs* down the lift shaft becomes a form of fucking play to them! They've been chucking the dead down that shaft for years now. They get a real kick when one is hurled over, but the corpses are nearly getting up to this floor so I guess the fuckers will be moving soon!"

Saskia felt nauseous after seeing the shaft of rotting flesh, but Levene's exuberant shout helped dispel this feeling. The pair had been hoping to find some males with energy left in them and when Marcia sighted six comparatively healthy specimens coming down the steps to their level she felt that they had struck gold!

"Now it's our playtime Sas – choose your fucking Stag!"

Levene raced up to the group – who were oblivious to anything but pleasure. The men ranged in age from late teens to mid-thirties. Marcia pounced on one of the younger guys whilst her partner started to rip the clothes off the oldest male. Smiles of total submission emanated from their victims and as both females started to arouse the genital area of their targets, a hedonistic orgy started to develop. The men would do anything that the women desired and the women were determined to *squeeze every ounce of sex* from them!

After Saskia had stripped her man naked, she

orally stimulated his penis and then roughly pushed him over. The man laughed, enjoying the game that he felt he was playing. The woman told him to lie still and then she knelt over him, impaling herself on his large phallus. Rivette's short skirt was forced up her lean stomach and then she started to claw the chest of the male until blood tracks appeared. Three other males watched the pair copulating and when he came, Rivette decided to increase the number of *players*. She forced a fresh male to the floor and started to glide her tongue across the girth of his penis. At the same time, she instructed a standing male to kneel and penetrate her from behind.

The three got into a rhythm that greatly magnified the sexual urges running through them. Rivette's head bobbed up and down whilst the kneeling male penetrated her anus. When she came, she savagely bit down on the floored male. She then swallowed both blood and semen. Saskia relaxed a little at this point and splayed her forearms on the floor whilst raising her arse higher in the air. Her second male shot his semen inside her and the woman turned over to *load her gun*.

Meanwhile Levene had ravished her younger victim with manic passion. He had ejaculated very quickly, before falling asleep in a light slumber. This premature climax had angered Marcia and she hungrily pulled an older male on top of her to try and satisfy her carnal needs. The *replacement* had a penis of some size with an unusual curvature and he managed a *deep* penetration that prompted a massive orgasm in the project woman. Levene lay idle for a few seconds, before kicking the male off her and joining Saskia as she loaded her weapon. Between them the pair had *roughly* acquired sex from four Prerogative Three victims, but their insatiable appetite for sex meant that they wouldn't be satisfied until they had experienced the two untried Stags.

The pair decided to carry out their first *kill* before their last bout of sex and so each woman pulled one of their previous partners to them; French-kissed their quarry and then shot the man through the heart whilst his tongue was still in their mouth! Both women had a symmetrical blood-stain on their upper garments after this callous act, but the surviving *bliss-slaves* just continued smiling at the killers – with nothing breaking their *contented* daze.

After attaching their *branding tags* to their victims, Marcia and Saskia moved in the direction of the two untried males. Rivette cast a loving look in Levene's direction and was about to say something to her, when she was shot where she stood! The bullet went clean through her head and as she fell for the last time, her blood bathed the concrete surface of floor five.

When Marcia Levene had heard the gunshot she instinctively dived for cover. The woman had quickly dropped to the floor and had spread-eagled herself behind one of the two males that she and Rivette had killed. She had looked back in time to see her partner waver and fall with her blood spraying in all directions.

The shot had been fired from the halfway-point on the stairs between floors five and six, but there wasn't anyone there now. Levene lay flat on the floor waiting to be shot at or verbally *challenged* in some way. Marcia assumed that rival taggers had attacked Saskia, but as the minutes ticked by, the silence wasn't broken. After half an hour in a cold sweat the woman could stand the silence no longer and then she issued a challenge of her own.

"Come on fuckers; show me your ugly faces. I'll drop the lot of you!"

Still the silence prevailed and then the woman snapped. She stood amidst the carnage and *spat* a venomous insult up the stairs.

"You fucking cowards! I wouldn't waste my piss on your fucking white feathers. Where's your fucking guts now?"

After her last tirade, Levene *did* hear a voice, but it wasn't the kind of *riposte* that she had expected.

"Go Levene. I don't want to *abort* your *presence.*"

Marcia was rendered dumb-struck by the utterance. She was scared that the person on floor six knew her identity and the tone of the voice was so deep that it almost sounded *non-human*. The speaker had slurred the word presence so that the *s* letter reverberated around their location and malevolence had shaped the word *abort*. Levene breathed in deeply to try and steady her resolve, but then a repugnant aroma filled her lungs.

As the smell became overpowering, she moved toward the stairs and then the *temperature* started to drop quite significantly. She could see her breath in the air around her and this uncanny factor helped make her mind up – with regard to evasive action. The woman had never run from a fight before, especially a *revenge* opportunity – but this was different. Her foe was unseen and supernatural elements seemed to surround his identity.

Her courage snapped and she raced down the stairs. On her way down, she distinctively heard the sound of a child laughing. The laughter echoed eerily around the concrete structure.

After Levene's departure, the four remaining Prerogative Three males crowded round Saskia's body. They wanted to *play* again and began removing all the dead woman's clothes. She had shown them a new game, one that made them feel wonderful. All

63

four of them wanted to feel that way again and *fill* their new *friend* with whiteness. As two of the males penetrated the corpse, a black irony began to take place, where Saskia's body was literally *Necsexed*!

When the four males had finished with Saskia's body, they descended the stairs leaving the corpse behind. Shortly after their departure, another series of footsteps could be heard coming *down* to floor five. A figure approached the body, touched some of the congealed blood on the forehead and inserted a branding tag through the flesh of the left breast. The tag carried a new name – *Klue.*

The *devil* still had another visit to make on that late-May evening. It involved a second audience with Jess Wheeler. Klue had decided that it was time that the MC-Project *front-line* protagonists visited their European counterparts again and after a little torture, Wheeler had been persuaded to organise plans for a project residence in Germany. He had started to pull the project closer to his *lair*!

seven

10 June was Feyer's birthday, but the Avoiders had never let celebrations break the routine of their fight for survival. When Feyer's small unit had fragmented from the main Harz pack, she had preserved the climate of abstinence and the woman had managed her three Avoiders with a rather puritan aloofness.

She looked at her reflection in the cracked mirror that was hung on the cellar wall. The daylight was only faint in the shadow-realm that she lived in, but she could still discern her painfully thin physique and the scar that marked her face. The woman felt miserable. After her nightmare, she had decided to venture out during daylight hours, despite her initial fears of being recognised by the MC-Project. She didn't join the others in the queue for provisions, opting to wander the outskirts of Goslar instead.

Feyer managed to obtain food for her pack in her role as a loan scavenger and her successes often matched the collective haul of her fellow Avoiders. She was contemplating which area of town to raid when a voice disturbed her.

"Hi Feyer, I've got you something."

The woman turned around to see Blackwell standing in the doorway to her cellar area. He was holding a small package in his hand. Her *stern* leadership qualities came to the fore as Feyer defensively interacted with Blackwell.

"What have you got me? Are you talking about provisions or what?"

"No - screw survival for one minute Feyer. I've got something for you."

"What the fuck for? Presents went out with the fucking ark you know. Who the hell wants to give gifts in our cesspool of an existence?"

"I do."

The couple fell silent for a moment and then Blackwell nervously handed his pack leader the wrapped package. He had broken Avoider protocol by breaking into a boarded-up jewellery shop instead of the disused food stores that provided essential items. His *heart* had ruled his actions in this instance. He knew the date of Feyer's birthday when he had asked her during their previous liaison and as the woman unwrapped the Amethyst necklace he waited for her hard exterior to bite.

"I'm right out of dinner parties at the moment Blackwell! When the fuck am I going to wear this?"

"In my dreams."

The answer knocked the woman back. The sincerity through which it was said represented a golden moment in a grey landscape and for a second the briefest of smiles flickered on the woman's face. Feyer then returned to her defensive nature, although by using Blackwell's Christian name, her *true* feelings were indicated.

"Born too late Dean! I don't quite figure out how Amethysts fit in with survival provisions, but ok – for a second you've cracked your *Ice-Maiden*. Now I'm sorry, but I've got to scour the maps of Goslar, so that I can re-route you three when you hit the food stores. We can't keep hitting the same areas because they'll smell us out if we get locked in a routine."

Dean persisted in his romantic interplay.

66

"Are you going to wear it for a second Feyer? Can I fasten it around your neck?"

The woman looked to the heavens and released an exasperated sigh. Once again she attempted to dampen down Blackwell's *fires* of attraction.

"For fucks sake Blackwell! Two questions! No and no – ok?"

"Fine Feyer. Just *keep* the necklace then, so you can think of me on dark lonely nights!"

The pair laughed – a rare sound to hear amongst Avoiders. The woman then playfully punched Blackwell and when he started to spar back, he turned awkwardly, slipped and fell arse-first to the cellar floor. The fall temporarily winded him, but his cheeky grin soon returned when he saw Feyer doubled up with laughter. He tried to squeeze his rare advantage.

"Any chance of a walk on the *lower* slopes, group-leader?"

The warm-hearted impudence of Blackwell made the woman drop to her knees with further bursts of laughter. Eventually she recovered her senses and spoke again. Her pragmatic sense of duty returned, but she had been softened.

"Get *real* Dean! What the hell are you on about? Who the fuck goes walking nowadays?"

"More people than you think. The three of us have found out a lot about the lives of the *wasted*, when we've joined ranks with them during the day.

"Look, can I show you what I mean?"

"What about the others?"

"They're already out on their Goslar beat. I told them that I was going to cover a different section of Goslar today."

"You've got it all figured out Dean haven't you? I guess it's years since anyone wished me a happy fucking birthday. This is a one off though Mr

67

Blackwell. I seem to remember saying that once before, but I mean it this time. If my *rank* stays here when I walk with you, it must remain our pact and when we return to this cellar, my status will likewise return. Are we agreed?"

"Yes."

After Feyer put on a headscarf to cover her distinctive black hair, the pair left their Goslar residence. They walked a few metres apart when they were in the streets of town, but this distance was reduced when they started to walk across the pasture that led onto the lower Harz slopes.

When Feyer and Blackwell walked through the lush grass, they started to feel a sense of *release* and a mutual bonding. They were now walking parallel to each other with only a few inches between them. Dean Blackwell turned to look at his colleague and she flashed a rare smile in his direction. Feyer then decided to take charge of the situation. She grabbed the man's left wrist and moved across him to bring their walk to a temporary halt. The woman placed both hands around the back of Blackwell's neck and he gently lowered his head to meet her narrow lips. As Feyer's eyes closed her soft tongue gently traced the contours of Blackwell's bottom lip and then both of them entered into a deep embrace.

The pair had kissed for a couple of minutes when approaching sounds interrupted them. Coming towards the couple were up to a hundred of the wasted Prerogative Three victims. At first Feyer was puzzled by the ordered procession, but then Blackwell shed some light on the anomaly.

"This is what I was on about Feyer. They walk the lower slope pastures everyday, whatever the weather. It's almost as if they are answering a *calling* of some kind. I know that the *bliss-slaves* are *shot-away* neurologically speaking, but what you're about to

witness will make you think for a moment. Their *ignorance* of anything evil has given them a naïve collective beauty. Watch you'll see what I mean."

The couple remained locked in each other's arms as the wasted generations started to file past them. Most didn't speak to Feyer or Blackwell, although the isolated few murmured *beautiful* as they went by them. Every single Prerogative Three victim shared one commonality – proffering the *familiar* diminished smile when they saw the pair. Towards the end of the procession, a small number of children flitted amongst the adults and for a few brief moments, Feyer regretted the self-abortion that she had undertaken.

When the last person had past them by, Blackwell spoke again.

"We'll give them a few minutes Feyer and then you'll be able to see the wasted in their playground."

The procession continued to walk up a rough track through the pasture and had shortly, collectively disappeared into the dense waist-high undergrowth. The pair started to follow in their footsteps and as they held hands, unfamiliar warmth started to glow in the heart of Feyer. Neither of them spoke to each other because they didn't want to arrest the silence that echoed the intensity of their new-found sanctuary. The track started to become steeper, until a little summit was reached. When Feyer looked downwards she saw a view that was so beautiful, it took her breath away.

The *wasted* had found their nirvana adjacent to a small pool on the fringes of a fir copse. Some of them swam in the deeper water, whilst others decorated fir trees with the dark purple flowers that were dotted all around them. The children tried to make garlands for their hair and they let out a shrill laughter when they were thwarted with the difficulty of the task. The scene reminded Feyer of some of her childhood memories. In a way the view in front of her held even more significance though, because it involved universal participation when compared to her domestic memories. It was a *natural celebration of life* in a world that had been soured by perversion.

After the couple had surveyed the *wasted* for a short time, Blackwell pulled Feyer down the grass slope toward the pool where some adults were bathing. When they reached the bank of the pool Dean started to shed his clothing and intimated through his eyes that Feyer should do the same. She laughed at Blackwell's obvious non-verbal innuendo and then started to join him in the act of undressing. The pair entered the water and stood amongst the ranks of the *wasted*, feeling pure in their nakedness.

Feyer dived underwater and was joined by Blackwell at the bottom of the pool. As the pair held their breath, they linked arms and exchanged tongues for a fleeting moment. Then both of them returned to the surface and bobbed up and down whilst extended French kissing took place. One of the wasted crashed into the pair in mid-embrace, but all three of them laughed off the collision – two through *reason* and one through *delirium*. Feyer then decided to initiate the next move. She felt warm between her legs despite the chilled water.

"I guess I'm in the mood to thaw down my barriers for a moment Dean. Do you want to re-enact our one yesterday in that fir copse over there?"

"I've been praying for that line Feyer – I thought I'd blown my chances."

"No you haven't. Spontaneity doesn't come easy for me you know! I'll be your *ice maiden* as soon as we hit Goslar again so I guess that this is my way of saying *take me while you can!*"

As the couple left the water, they linked hands and headed for their evergreen sanctuary. They remained naked and when they contacted the verdant covering of the copse floor, Feyer felt like the first couple for a brief instant. The sounds of laughter and joviality were now muted as the throng was a hundred meters away and the seclusion of their evergreen retreat gave them a private intimacy. This feeling increased the sexual undercurrent that existed between them and as they lay on their evergreen carpet, love consumed them. This was a *first* for Feyer.

When the pair had *traded* tongues in the pool Feyer had felt raunchy, even mildly decadent as the nakedness around her had hade her feel as though she was partaking in an orgy of sorts. Now that she and Blackwell were alone together, this feeling had altered to take on a much more *deep* satisfaction. He ran his hands down her back, using gentle strokes that were the antithesis of the *wild* groping that the pair had previously inflicted on each other. Sex on that one previous occasion had been good, but it had been delivered via lust with any love being an absent stranger. As Blackwell moved on top of the woman she parted her legs, gradually at first, but wider when she was ready for him. She started to rhythmically anticipate her penetration by raising her arse some inches from the copse floor. Dean made her wait for a few seconds longer, not wanting the cherished liaison to end too soon. He was savouring every moment and to him penetration would mark the beginning of the end. He knew that the old Feyer would sure enough come back when they returned to Goslar. She had stated that this would be the case and so Dean felt that further kissing could stall this transition and temporarily prolong his ecstasy.

Eventually though he too succumbed to

temptation and he gradually started to move inside Feyer. She let out a muffled gasp against his right cheek and the pair then devoured each other's tongues with heightened fervour. When Blackwell achieved full penetration, the pair engaged in an *athletic* bout of lovemaking that soon had sweat glistening on their faces.

Feyer was very wet between her legs and when Blackwell felt her dampness on the tops of his thighs, he knew that his ejaculation wouldn't be long in coming. His penetrative strokes then quickened and when Feyer *came* in a rhythmical frenzy, he followed suit, shooting his sperm deep into the woman he *loved*. During his climax, Blackwell had gently bitten into the woman's ear and his hot saliva had triggered another orgasm in his *temporary* lover. The pair lay silently in a state of mutual satisfaction. Dean wished that they could engage in a relationship of a more *lasting* significance, but he felt that their moral affinity wouldn't survive in the social pollution around them. He would always *dream* though, until his worst fears were realised.

Feyer was the first to stir from the light slumber that had claimed the lovers. She gently removed Blackwell's arms from her frame and then she stood, arching her back in the process. She smiled at the late-afternoon sunlight and reflected on the beautiful images she had seen that day. She could still discern sounds from the *paradise* in the lowland beneath the fir copse and then another sound entered her aural awareness. This sound was known to Feyer and it represented a *dark* antithesis to the laughter below her.

The *Apache Black-Slayer* was the latest attack helicopter to be utilised by the MC-Project and the drone of its rotor blades were instantly recognisable to those who feared pursuit. This had been the sound

that had cut through the laughter and the woman roughly awoke Blackwell, to tell him of the impending threat. The pair ran to the fringes of the copse and surveyed the approaching choppers. The craft seemed like *vultures* in movement and their black colour gave them another *sinister* dimension.

The two choppers started to approach the sky above the lower slopes, where the *wasted* still bathed. Feyer tightly grasped Blackwell's arm as she deduced the heinous action that was going to take place.

Their collective nakedness had given the pair a quasi-innocence before, but now it represented vulnerability for the couple. The copse was even more of a sanctuary now and although both of them initially wanted to warn the bliss-slaves of the military killing-machine coming their way, the wasted hadn't retained mental comprehension of *anything negative*. Subsequently their warnings wouldn't make any sense to the ranks of the innocent. Even *evasive* action would be an *alien* concept to them!

The two helicopters moved over the lower slopes and hovered directly above the bathers. The noise was quite tumultuous and the downwind whipped up small waves on the surface of the pool. The craft were less than forty metres above the ranks of the wasted when the firing started. Feyer and Blackwell had returned to their sick planet.

The choppers could easily have undertaken the massacre in less than twenty seconds, but the four pilots were on a *sport-cruise* and were determined to savour every ounce of the bloodshed. The co-pilots had opted to use powerful game-rifles and the slow reload factor associated with this weapon would prolong the agony for Blackwell and Feyer. One of the craft had the tag-name 'Skum 10' daubed on the side of it and it was the co-pilot of this chopper who claimed first-blood in the killing spree.

The powerful hunting rifle unleashed a three-inch shell that went straight through the eye socket of a sixty –year-old woman. The trajectory of this bullet continued after the initial impact and smashed the hip-bone of a teenage onlooker. Feyer screamed at the evil that had taken over the sky.

"You're the spawn of the devil, you fucking cunts! Jeez Dean – the bastards are going to *slow-kill* the entire lot!"

Feyer was correct. That was exactly what the four pilots had in mind and as the massacre continued both she and Blackwell found that they couldn't turn away from the killing spree. The pair weren't morbidly curious; they just found the horror so *overwhelming* following the beauty that they had recently shared. Their paradise had effectively been *raped* by the MC-Project – the scourge of what was left of society. The co-pilot in the untagged chopper eventually tired of his single shot weapon and he started to spray machine-gun fire down at the targets of innocence.

As the *wasted* bodies started to pile up, areas of verdant pasture grass became red with the deluge of blood. The *wasted* remained oblivious to the threat, pointing up at the choppers with smiles on their faces. They even made gesticulations to each other, mimicking the rotor blades as they sped round. The pilots laughed at this ignorance, especially the *guest* co-pilot who had come to witness the *sport*. He was enjoying his European placement and had specifically asked to become involved in a massacre of the wasted. He wanted to see the fruits of his hard labours paying dividends. He was after all the author of the plans behind the destruction of the wasted. None other than David Tavini was the guest in question! The MC-Project front-liner was in his

element as he partook in the *slaughter*. He sprayed machine gun bullets down at the ground with a wild abandon, laughing manically as his victims fell. He killed a mother, father and young daughter in one particularly devastating burst of fire and his fellow pilot slapped him on the back, heartily applauding his accuracy. Tavini couldn't resist a callous comment to *celebrate* his murder of a family unit.

"Call me *Mr three-in-one* Raz! I'm fucking *primed* for killing out here. Jeez I fucking love life. Did you see their pathetic smiling faces when I made them *eat lead?* Viva *our new - world* pal! We'll eventually get bored of this sitting-duck target practice, but right now it's heaven man!"

Feyer slumped down against a fir-tree. There was nothing that she or Blackwell could do. They were both still naked, without any guns to hand to fire back at the helicopters. They also knew that they carried the visual location of their colleagues back in Goslar – in their main MC vaults. There was no choice, but to sit out the massacre.

Eventually just the Apaches could be heard and the craft then simultaneously started to gain altitude. The choppers did a final *once-over* of the massacre location, before beginning the flight back to *Designation base M* in Hanover. This was the appointed venue for the temporary residence of the American front–line division.

After the choppers had departed, Feyer and Blackwell left the copse. They had got to collect their clothing and provision bags from the banks of the bathing pool. As the pair went down the hillside a sight of extreme devastation met their eyes. The *wasted* lay dead all around them, splayed out on the grass and an unnatural *silence* was the background for each *portrait* of death. Feyer had hoped to find *some* people who had escaped the summary executions, but in her heart she knew that *each* person had lost the ability for *reasoned flight* due to the neurological alterations that had been performed upon them. Death had subsequently claimed the totality of the group. When the pair walked amidst the corpses, they started to reclaim their belongings. Fresh blood soiled the garments in both cases and each Avoider fought against the mounting nausea inside them. One image eventually made Feyer fall to her knees and sob at the evil that had taken place. Two infants lay slain, holding hands with smiles of apparent *release* on their faces. Both had garlands in their hair and this image of juvenile peace rocked Feyer to her core. She stared savagely back to the copse of *intimacy* and let her anger achieve a form of catharsis through Blackwell's presence.

"Do you see where love has got us Dean? Side-tracked us, into escaping this fucking carnage. I'll *spit* on love if this is the battering card! Christ I wish something could blow the fuck out of our blackened planet."

The two pilots of the *untagged* helicopter were having quite a different type of conversation on their way back to Hanover. Raz and Tavini had continued to extol each other's fighting prowess and were *pumped* even higher on the massacre, then when they were actually implementing the bloodshed. Raz turned to David and offered the front-liner a tab of *Icerlikx* – just one of the performance drugs that most of the MC-Project now consumed on a daily basis. He was desperate to urinate and decided to give his *superior* a challenge that he knew he wouldn't refuse.

"I'm bursting to go *back-afters* Mr Tavini. Are you man enough to sit in the main seat of a *Black-Slayer* all on your *own-some* or is that a false bravado on your face?"

Tavini could never resist a challenge to the man the controls of the latest military technology and so he took the *hot-seat*, after sending Raz away with a playful punch on his back.

He soon became immersed in controlling the powerful Attack-Helicopter and didn't initially notice the *new* presence that sat down in the seat next to him. When Tavini turned round the occupant had dropped his black altitude – visor over his face. He started to gauge something was wrong when the *much taller* occupant spoke to him.

"*Leanworld* passed on David. That's good, as things should be. No need now David. No need for *you* that is. You've painted a *beautiful* tapestry you know – *our purgatory* on earth. I have loved your work David – thank you."

With that remark Klue's left-gloved hand gently closed over David Tavini's right and a piercing scream reverberated throughout the helicopter. Tavini hadn't felt any pain, but when he had glanced down to where his right hand used to be, he just saw the frozen entrails that a *Klue-handshake* left as a *calling-card*. Tavini *then* felt the pain that the image deserved and as the craft plummeted, the pressure forced him to the floor. Hundreds of images fought for dominance in Tavini's *mindsight* vault, but all were wiped by his *final* recollection. His co-pilot had partially raised his visor to reveal an overlarge glutinous mouth that salivated in the expectation of Tavini's death. This was to be the last thing that David Tavini saw and just before the *flames*, the lips enclosed on him to proffer a *satanic benediction*.

eight

After the massacre on the lower slopes, Feyer had
initially sunk into depression. She had carried on with
her leadership duties, but nihilism had entered her
psyche and she remained quiet in the extreme. At
night she would replay the atrocity in her mind over
and over again, trying to determine if she and
Blackwell could have done anything to prevent the
massacre. Once a week had elapsed, she knew that
her guilt was unfounded and she started to look at life
on slightly more favourable terms. The woman
concentrated on where she could relocate her pack.
She had witnessed the deaths of over three hundred
people in two Goslar killing sprees and after scouring
maps of their locale, Feyer had decided that she
would move her Avoiders closer to the town of
Hamelin. She hadn't told the others about her
relocation plans yet, but she felt that the relocation
should take place within the next week. All four
Avoiders had started to venture out into the streets of
Goslar together now, breaking with the separation
logic that had previously been adhered to. As the four
walked the cobbled streets on that particular morning,
fate was waiting to spin its web.

Danny Seaton had remained in Goslar since the
massacre in the market square. He had been placed
on a compulsory leave period, after a female Avoider

had killed his fellow laser cannon operator.

Boredom had now started to set in and as he aimlessly walked the streets of Goslar, he longed for the day when his MC-Project paymasters would allow him back on active duty. As he kicked the litter in the street, some of the wasted passed him. He idly scanned a few of their faces and after a further batch of four had passed him by, a vengeful look came over him. He had *recognised* a woman – the killer of his partner!

Seaton was tempted to claim the *glory* immediately and wipe the four as they walked away, but he decided to adhere to project protocol instead – feeling that this would speed up his return to active duty. He subsequently went into a side-street, turned on his comm.-lynx and contacted his section leader to tell him whom he had just seen.

"I've just spotted the female Avoider who took out the Kaiserworth Mr Heston!"

"What is the code setting?"

"Goslar – Area 23. There's three more with her, two males and one femme."

"Follow at a discreet distance. Don't let them suss that you're armed. We want this woman *alive* Seaton – you hear me *alive*! No fucking shoot-outs this time – you hear me?"

"That's crystal Mr Heston. How long until an arrest-squad arrive?"

"They'll be with you in less than thirty. Start pursuit Seaton. Wire out."

Seaton deactivated his comm.-lynx and then started to follow the four Avoiders. As he threaded his way through the ranks of the wasted he kept looking ahead for Feyer's headscarf. By *fixing* her presence, he could account for the others and he was determined that this time his quarry would not evade him. After twenty-five minutes of slow-tracking, he could hear the faint siren of a project security vehicle. This wasn't an unusual sound to hear in Goslar, but as the vehicle got nearer to his vicinity Seaton's pulse quickened. *His* moment had arrived. He had been so long in the back line, just a numbered employee – now they would have to notice him. Seaton didn't like his pompous line – leader and he was determined to make the arrest himself otherwise others would grab *his glory*. If that transpired he would remain hidden amongst the ranks of the mundane and Seaton hated mediocrity. He thirsted for the kill.

When the security vehicle arrived at the end of their street the Avoiders broke into two pairs. Feyer and Blackwell ran down a side-street. She had given the order to break, because she knew that the vehicle was patrolling in a systematic fashion, with a quarry in mind. The laboured speed and the surveillance personnel on the roof of the vehicle proved that and subsequently Feyer reasoned that retreat was their best option. The four of them could have *played dumb* like the wasted souls around them, but the woman realised that she would be on the wanted visual-file, as a second-in-command Avoider. This factor would have been ascertained by the project through scanning the memory-vaults of the *dead-heads* previously left in Goslar. The others probably wouldn't have been logged by the project and thus she called for the split to protect her three subordinates. She had told Blackwell to escape with Ludmilla and Matthew Reed, but he had followed Feyer – wanting to share in her sacrificial gesture.

The vehicle registered the split and it accelerated quickly down the side-street. This prompted Ludmilla and Reed to panic and quicken the pace of their retreat from the vehicle. Unfortunately that meant that they raced straight in the direction of *glory-boy*!

Bullet one tore off half of Ludmilla's face and bullet two-pierced Matthew Reed's heart. Feyer's pack now numbered two!

Feyer and Blackwell tore down the side-street, but the security vehicle was on their heels in a matter of seconds. The driver *cruelly* slowed down to a pace, just a mite slower than the two runners. He kept this up until the pair was boxed down another side-street without any exit routes. Tall three-storey buildings flanked the street on either side and when the pair reached the end of the street, their luck had finally run out. They looked upwards to see a ten-metre high, red-brick wall. Then they turned on their tracks and faced the advancing security vehicle. The pair did have pistols, but these would be absolutely useless against the impregnable surface of the bullet-proof vehicle. Feyer looked at Blackwell and suicide momentarily flickered in her eyes Then a cold voice sounded from the vehicle.

"Throw down your weapons. Your race has ended. Resistance equals death."

The hooded surveillance troops on top of the vehicle added to the dark presence that the pair had felt when the mechanistic, amplified voice had sounded from the vehicle.

The wind-screen of the vehicle was tinted to an optimum level and so neither Feyer nor Blackwell could make out the occupants inside. Feyer knew that escape was impossible, but her tenacious spirit returned and she eradicated any thoughts of turning the gun on herself. In a typical show of defiance she hurled the weapon at the vehicle. Blackwell then followed suit.

"Spread yourself scum. A false move releases our trigger fingers."

Feyer and Blackwell did as they had been

commanded and when they were face down in the
dirt, three of the hooded surveillance crew climbed
down from the vehicle to undertake body searches on
the pair. All three were male and Feyer wasn't
surprised when they dwelled over her search. The
groping fingers were just another sick symptom of
their decaying world. The woman had tied the
Amethyst necklace that Blackwell had given her to
the inside lining of her ragged shirt, but a surveillance
officer ripped it apart without a second glance. The
gem-stones were thrown aside and when she was
allowed to stand after her search was over, she
initially tried to reclaim them. A rifle butt to the back
of her head put paid to any reclamation and Feyer
was hurled into the security vehicle unconscious. The
couple were sedated in the vehicle and they were
oblivious when they were transferred to a gunship
helicopter. The destination of the craft was Hanover –
where Blackwell and Feyer would have an audience
with some of the American MC-Project cohort!

In the Hanover Designation Wheeler had seen
visual glimpses of Feyer's role in the Kaiserworth
demolition. Clancy's decapitated head had been
retrieved and the Memory-Camera vaults of this grisly
discovery provided images of the woman dragging
explosive material into the building. Other Avoider
heads had been explored and Feyer had frequently
been *visually hallmarked* as an Avoider of some
importance. Wheeler had first felt uneasy when he
saw Feyer's face and the spirit in her eyes. There was
something about her that seemed to convey a
presence that was intangible – a factor that set her
apart from the other bedraggled Avoiders. The
shadow of Klue had perpetually hung over Wheeler,
since their first meeting and yet even his satanic
presence seemed to momentarily weaken when Jess
first saw Feyer on the laser screen. He had imposed a

high-priority status with regard to her capture and
fate had dealt him the successful completion of his
edict, far sooner than he had anticipated.

Levene had also witnessed the laser screening and
she had been impressed with the resilience that the
woman demonstrated. She had said to Wheeler that
the MC-Project could use a woman of such tenacity.
Wheeler had initially agreed, although he was more
guarded with praise because he wasn't sure what his
secret rein-handler would think. He also saw through
Marcia to a level, feeling that it wasn't just Feyer's
mind that Levene wanted to *get inside*!

The American division had been devastated by the
loss of David Tavini. When his helicopter had failed
to return, a massive search was embarked upon and
the tangled wreckage was eventually found. Some of
the American division journeyed to the site in the vain
hope that Mr *America* would spring phoenix-like from
the scene of the crash. As soon as they saw the
scattered debris, each of them had to acknowledge
the truth – David Tavini was *dead* and never coming
back. Levene and Wheeler had formally identified
Tavini's body. This had been a difficult task, because
there had been precious little left to identify.
Eventually the pair acknowledged the remains to be
those of their former colleague, thanks largely to the
distinctive necklace that David had always worn. One
bizarre factor that Levene couldn't account for was
the shards of ice that were evident throughout the
wreckage. She asked Wheeler about this anomaly, but
he hadn't clarified the matter beyond some vague
comments about atmospheric conditions at a higher
altitude. Despite his professed ignorance regarding
this matter, Wheeler knew exactly what the ice
represented. The shards were the same kind of long,
barbed splinters that Klue had left behind after their

first meeting. The shards were unmistakably *his* work. Wheeler shivered when the enormity of this act sank home - *his* satanic visitor had destroyed David. Jess was starting to realise *that evil had levels*!

Marcia had taken Tavini's death very hard. She would miss his friendship and the intense S&M sessions that she had enjoyed with him. She had probably felt a form of love for David, albeit a type that had *savagery* seal the bonding. Levene thrived on deviant sexual practises and Tavini had reciprocated her sting. After four days she came out of her self-imposed isolation and gradually started to feel her way back into front-line work.

Her *predatory* instincts also returned on a sexual level and when she first saw Feyer on the laser screen a few days later, dark lust *tethered* her desire. She knew that Wheeler had recognised this factor as soon as she had seen the screen. His eyes had seemed to read her indulgent reflections.

Once Levene heard that Feyer had been captured and imprisoned in the very building where she had a temporary residence, it didn't take her long to make her first visit. She went alone and found her quarry tied down on an iron prison bed. Feyer had been isolated from Blackwell and the woman scowled at Levene when she made her entrance. The MC-Project woman ignored this factor and took the verbal lead.

"I guess you're quite a find Feyer! Some of your comrades *framed* you quite well in their MC-vaults, but you're much more *elfin* in the flesh – more enticing shall we say. Sorry about the Spartan accommodation, but I guess this is a palace when compared to the hovels that you usually take residence in! Can I get you anything?"

"Fuck you!"

"I may have had something similar in mind, but let's not rush things shall we?"

THE SCREAM OF FEYER

Feyer bristled at Levene's play on her words. She had hated the image of the smartly dressed project woman as soon as she came into her room, but her insinuation really brought fire into Feyer's eyes. Levene continued.

"Here we are – two women at opposite ends in the land of opportunity! You with cut knees and a scarred face: me with my ultimate power – cards and selected hand – servants. It's funny how the dice falls isn't it Feyer? Funny how you ended up at the *begging-bowl* end of society with your *waspish* good looks."

Marcia paused for a moment before moving closer to Feyer's bed. Her eyes scanned the ragged clothes on the woman as she lay on top of the meagre sheets that covered her bed. She moved within inches of Feyer's face and spoke in a soft whisper that was untypical of her usual resonant utterances.

"I guess that this is as close as people get to you isn't it Feyer? After the project's sojourn to Paris in four days time, we will dip into your *mindsight* to fathom what really drives you: reveal the *real* Feyer and the intimacy that defines her spirit. I'll be a voyeur on the front seat then, but until that moment I suppose that I have to make do with small encounters to staunch my indulgent spirit. I've decided to clean you up a bit today and get rid of those fucking awful rags that obscure the waif underneath!"

Levene reached into her shoulder bag and Feyer squirmed uneasily, trying to break free from the thick leather straps that pinned her to the bed. The MC-Project woman ignored her futile resistance and proceeded to take a bone-handled knife from her bag. The blade was very sharp and when Levene raised the knife higher in the air, a *devilish* smile briefly flickered on her face. This prompted Feyer to speak. Her words still had a tone of defiance, but she was fearful of Levene's intentions and her voice subsequently lacked power.

"Why don't you get it over with? One clean stab wound, wipe the blood on the sheets and one more Avoider will be extinguished!"

"I've told you Feyer. I've come here to tidy you up, not to fucking slaughter you. I'll show you what the knife is for."

Levene started to pull Feyer's rags from her and if the material was tougher than she expected, the knife was utilised. In just under a minute Marcia had cut the ragged clothing away, leaving her quarry naked. The black leather straps provided an interesting tonal contrast to Feyer's pale flesh.

The project woman reached inside her back again and took out some materials that she had brought along for Feyer's *cleansing*. As she began rubbing a powerful soap into the pores of Feyer's skin, she continued to speak to her strapped-down target.

"I'm going to relax you Feyer. I bet you haven't been *pampered* for years. All you have got to do is shut your beautiful eyes and surrender to my touch. This will be therapeutic for both of us you know. I'll get off by skin-rinsing a beautiful woman and you'll experience a form of massage that will blow your fucking mind."

Feyer recoiled at Levene's words and she spat back a riposte.

"I've never been a *femme-to-femme* sexual player. Why the hell should I start now?"

"Lighten up woman! You haven't got much fucking choice in the matter anyway have you?"

"You know as a woman, that I can easily freeze you off by tightening *those* muscles and *blanking* your words."

"You won't though. At least if you have any regard for your final pack member next door. I can easily

make a jewellery-bag out of his scrotum with this knife and I fucking will do if you piss me off by opting for a non-reaction."

Feyer knew that Levene was *savage* with lust and she could easily imagine the woman taking the knife to Blackwell. One solitary tear escaped from her shut-eyes, as she turned her head tighter into her pillow. Levene saw this reaction and for the first time in years, she felt a form of pity. Her next words were subsequently gentler, being similar to some of the dialogue that she had shared with Saskia Rivette.

"Listen Feyer. I keep losing people who are close to me. For once I guess that I'm ready to occupy a quieter corner – to temporarily tame my ferocious existence. You see right now my heart is crying out for simple pleasures. Is lathering your hair and anointing your skin such a crime? In the context of what I could do to you? In four days time I will go to Paris with the other front-liners. We are going to celebrate the fifth anniversary of Mr Wheeler's tenure in the highest project office. He is our ultimate leader and the *masquerade-ball* that is planned, will be the perfect way to congratulate him. We recently lost a brilliant front-liner and Mr Wheeler seemed to lose his usual energy a short while ago when we were in the States. When all things are considered, a few dark clouds seem to be gathering on our project horizon. I want calm if another storm awaits us and spending a few hours of relaxation with you partly restores my inner-peace."

Levene's reflections had allowed her *softer* side to briefly shine through and although Feyer still feared the project woman, she didn't feel as though her life was in immediate jeopardy any longer. Feyer let her mind wander to distant memories as Levene's hands set to work. She didn't leave any area untouched and her vigorous finger-work had a power that was firm yet strangely soothing. Feyer tensed as the hands neared her genital area, but when Levene reached her pubic mound she didn't alter her method of coverage, or spend longer on that region of Feyer's body. Marcia did want to penetrate Feyer with one or more of her fingers, but with the exception of one brief forefinger stroking motion, she managed to resist her temptations!

After Levene had finished massaging Feyer's body, she turned her attention to the woman's face and hair. The long fingers were utilised to apply a form of pressure that intensified at the apex of her cranium. A warm rushing feeling pulsated through Feyer and as Levene's method increased in pace, the heat started to fuse with the hypnotic rhythm generated by the finger-work. Feyer momentarily relaxed in an ambient dream-like state. She felt weightless and almost astral in terms of consciousness.

Her black hair was washed through twice with a shampoo that Levene normally reserved just for herself and her scalp tingled after this cleansing. After twenty minutes Feyer was eventually brought back to her state of restriction, when Levene started to undo the straps that bound her! The project woman spoke again after what had been quite a lengthy period of silence.

"Your co-operation has activated my *compassionate* side Feyer! Those who fight me suffer my vengeance, but those who have a more subservient relationship with me are treated well. I *tire* of being the dominatrix all the time and like a little brutalising myself on occasions! Today my *reward* for your partial-compliance, will involve taking your tether-straps away with me! You can have your room freedom, although still a bolted-room as I'm sure you'll understand! When I return from Paris we'll

take things a stage further, but until then this will
have to do!"

Levene savagely pulled Feyer to her and briefly
rammed her tongue into the woman's mouth. Feyer
was taken aback and didn't respond or pull away. As
the project woman rose to leave, Feyer flickered a
half-smile, grateful for the small-mercy of being able
to walk around her room.

That night Feyer initially slept well due to her
new-found freedom of movement, but at 04:33 she
was woken by an intense cold that had enveloped her
room. In the weak chink of lighting afforded by the
outside corridor, she could sense that she wasn't
alone. The voice of a young girl cut through the semi-
darkness.

"So cold. I'm so cold. I need a friend."

"Where are you?"

"Under your bed. Why do you *hate* me so – lady?
Why do you *kill* my kind?"

"I don't hate you. Let me see you. You can have
my blanket to warm yourself. Please let me see you."

The child crept out from under the bed and Feyer
could just discern the thinnest juvenile that she had
ever laid eyes on. She gasped in horror, trying to
reduce the audible nature of her shock. The child
spoke again.

"Those needles *hurt* you know. Ever realised that?
We're left red, dead and lonely – you know! Ever
realised that?"

Feyer froze when she realised that *somehow* the
child knew about the abortion that she had
undertaken. She felt sorrow and guilt, but also a form
of anger that her dark secret had been discovered.
Her uneasiness was evident in her next utterance.

"What I did was carried out in rugged pasture
many kilometres from here. How could you have

shared my privacy, when I was forced into *that* option? Anyway, how did you get into my room and where the hell are your parents?"

Feyer had been unnerved by the juvenile intrusion and she had asked several questions in a very short duration. When the child answered, she had another dark surprise waiting for her.

"You've met my Father in his kingdom. I'm surprised that you don't remember! Only for a short moment you understand, but my father just *isn't* forgotten by those who meet him."

Feyer had a horrible feeling that she was going to relive something *unpleasant*, but she hadn't linked all the pieces together yet. The woman was rapidly getting frustrated with the distant, childish-whine and her annoyance surfaced.

"Where *exactly* is your father? I want to see him."

"We are *one*. We are Klue. Do you remember those drowning fishermen, their bursting lungs and the stench of Hell? Do you remember gliding down? You saw Klue's plated-back didn't you? We all have questions – don't we *fucker*? *Never* demand an audience with Klue's bestial nature. You're just *shit on his claws*."

The *savage* change in the juvenile form of Klue terrified Feyer into silence. She realised that this creature was from another *darker* world and she now linked her current danger to her previous nightmare-journey. The pungent smell that had previously soiled her lungs returned, forcing the woman to double-up and vomit. The child started to laugh in an uncontrollable manner. It walked right up to Feyer's bed and delivered a final damnation, before fading through the darkness. The words stung.

"I guess mummy not feeling well now. Well suffer fucker – just like foetal entities! You *will* meet my Father, but you won't fucking thank *us* for the

pleasure!'

When the child had gone, Feyer walked around her *cell*. She trembled with fear, but at least the meeting had given her a form of clarity – proving that her vision had been a *real* experience. She wondered how many forms Klue could take and which one would seek her out next. Her constant walk *on the edge of a blade* was hardening the woman.

nine

As the early morning July sunlight bathed Paris, Jess Wheeler envisaged the day ahead of him. He had been MC-Project leader for half a decade now and the impending masquerade-ball that evening would honour his tenure. Klue hadn't visited Wheeler for several days and Jess was gradually starting to feel like he used to – although the satanic spectre hanging over him would never be far from his thoughts.

The man walked into his luxury-suite window and started to scan the landmarks that represented the *city of love*. The Eiffel Tower was the most impressively designed structure, although the Rochaux edifice was forty metres taller. This structure had been completed in 2008 and it meant that an MC-Project division looked down on the rest of Paris. The masquerade-ball was due to take place seven floors below Wheeler's suite in the retro-Baroque ballroom. *La Maison de l'Amour Noir* was the name of the selected venue and it was currently the favoured destination for intellectually-favoured Parisians. Although the venue had only been around for a few years, it had been designed on a site that had previously been associated with a darkened reputation. In the seventeenth century public executions had taken place on the site and then the area had become associated with witchcraft. The area had rightly acquired a reputation for ill-fortune and prostitutes gained sanctuary in the climate of fear that history

had generated. The erection of the current structure sought to dispel the suffering of the past if not the mystique. Indeed the name of the structure admirably *kissed* history.

Wheeler had to formally greet the MC-Project cohort, before the masquerade-ball could begin. The celebration was to be themed with clandestine liaisons proving the inspiration for the gathering on this occasion. Jess was looking forward to being the *master of dark ceremony*.

Whilst Jess Wheeler finished fine-tuning his introductory speech, the ballroom was being made ready for the big event. The high ceiling was encrusted with plaster spires that hung down in a stalactite fashion and blue-marble fragments were sunk into the plaster in a symmetrical pattern. Choice landscapes by Claude and Poussin appeared on the west-facing wall and mannequins in seventeenth century costumes flanked the opposite wall. Glass screens in painterly Baroque colours were evident on both sides of the ballroom entrance and a canted figure-of-eight conveyor belt was placed five metres above the floor. That evening the conveyor belt would carry living models that would keep the Baroque theme and intertwine erotic clandestine elements. The back wall had a huge holographic-fountain projected against it and that night, a full orchestra would be simulated through the fountain. Nothing would be deemed too grand to celebrate Jess Wheeler's five years in office. Everything pointed to another *overshow* of project opulence and as the ostentatious MC-ranks got ready for their evening, indulgent vanity was all around.

Marcia Levene was nearly ready for what she *knew* would be another decadent night of S&M-driven sex. As she finished preening her finery, she looked at

herself in a full – length mirror. She had opted to wear
a satin full-length black dress with a split up to her
hips on each side. She deliberately let the scars from
her Tavini sessions show through. These were of a
symmetrical nature running down each outer-thigh in
an S-pattern. As she remembered the violent sex that
she and David used to share, she became damp
between her legs. Those times had answered the
callings of her savage sexual gratification and her skin
longed for his type of lacerations!

Levene tried on her black leather face-mask. She
felt at home with the relative anonymity that the mask
provided. Her eyes and mouth were partially visible,
but soft layers of leather covered the rest of her face.
She would be *hunting Stags* that night! She hadn't felt
the pulsating veins of a penis inside her since
Necsexing with Saskia. Her vagina *ached* from under-
use.

Marcia then accentuated the fullness of her lips
applying a black-cherry lipstick. This colour brought
back good memories for her, of distant times and a
distant lover. She still *loved* being locked in her
vanity.

She looked at her dressing-table and laughed when
she saw a dark purple wig. She had played-along by
wearing it for the MC-Project several years ago and
she suddenly thought that it would add to her
masquerade if she wore it again. In just a few minutes
her new form of disguise was complete and a largely
unrecognisable Levene walked out of her room.

She chose to walk down the spiral- staircase. This
was glass-panelled and her descent could be seen
from outside the building, because the staircase was
appended to the outer-walls in a corkscrew-type
design. Levene knew that those arriving for the ball
would witness her gradual descent and she figured
that a lot of *hyper-sexed* males would be able to see

right up her – from their low-angle vantage point.

Marcia was still a *head-turner* in her forties and when she entered the ballroom, many gave her more than a second glance.

The leading global MC-Project personnel were in attendance and each of them had adhered to the masquerade dress code. The Chinese delegation had the most ornate facial masks and the said form of disguise compensated for what they collectively lacked in height. Their masks involved a black-leather base like Levene. Jewels and gold dragons were appended to the leather, making the overall effect more sumptuous than their global counterparts. Just fewer than two thousand project staff had received an invitation to the event and the ballroom was packed by their collective presence. As Wheeler approached the speakers' podium to formally open the masquerade ball, he cast a nervous glance over his shoulder at the massed ranks. Hope was returning to his dark heart and he wondered, just wondered – if Klue had left him for good! Confidence was thus gradually returning to the MC-Project leader and his opening words revealed his new-found strength.

"Five years on the throne of *paradise* my people! Five years of growth and success as we forge a better world. I may be at the helm, but I think all of you know that the captain is *nothing* without a crew to serve him and what a crew you are! Just over a month ago, one of our finest project players made the ultimate sacrifice for our beloved cause. David Tavini's death was a great loss to all of us, but his spirit lives on with each new milestone we accomplish. As a mark of respect for the great man, we decided to implement his Leanworld Vision the day after his remains were found.

"You will have already noticed the results of his

no-provision policy. Already the numbers of the *wasted* are significantly lower. Soon those who were totally dependent on our subsistence will be no more and the world will be a haven for the intellectually gifted. No one will be left to slow us down. Our perfect community has started!"

The man paused briefly to let his words strike home and then continued to extol Tavini's achievements.

"You see David is talking to us from his grave. His intellectual genius will get closer to *immortality* in terms of effect, as each member of the wasted withers and falls! His planning has paved the way for our dream-world and before we celebrate tonight we will initially bear the man the respect he deserves, by standing for three minutes of silent appreciation."

The requested silence was honoured to a person and then Wheeler spoke again.

"Tonight is our celebration. You will honour my five years in office by living the wild-culture of excess! This venue is yours, Do with it, as you will. Every room is open, every want provided for. Catch the Tavini-spirit and entertain yourselves like there's no fucking tomorrow! Go for it!"

When Jess Wheeler had finished, the virtual orchestra were activated through the huge back – wall fountain. The first piece played was well known amongst project ranks – a *Necrowaltz* entitled *The Love of the Black Horizon*. This piece set the requested decadent tone!

As soon as the *virtual orchestra* started to play, the conveyor-belt was put in motion. Initially the models adopted statuesque poses that mirrored the mannequins below them. They had drapes and sashes of Baroque colour schemes tied to their bodies and beneath the drapes each model wore skimpy black-latex undergarments. As the *Necrowaltz* started to

approach its zenith, the models started to writhe and
reach out for each other. They peeled off their sashes
and threw them down to the dancing crowd beneath
them. Then in pairs they started to cut each other out
of their latex undergarments. Each model moved
rhythmically, achieving choreographed harmony with
the piece played by the orchestra. In a short time each
model was naked and their sexual organs were
masturbated to a state of high arousal. Because the
conveyor-belt was angled at forty-five degrees, the
project ranks were treated to full-view voyeurism!
Occasionally a model would partially lose their
balance, but they always recovered due to their
professional agility. MC-Project staff had handpicked
each model and the chosen were putting on a sexual
performance of the highest quality. As the music
beneath them became more decadent the models
entered into a collective sexual frenzy. Each male was
forced to adhere to a *no-cum* policy, because the
audience were directly below him! Despite this factor,
a few released on the quiet when they were
penetrating a partner. Ejaculation was still viewed as
risky by the majority of performers though, because
they had been contracted for a twelve - hour shift with
just a few ten – minute rest periods.

The 'Shagfest' nature of this work always paid well
as large numbers of the intellectually-favoured
consistently expressed their appreciation for this type
of background entertainment. Thirty-six models had
been hired to perform for Mr Wheeler's big night and
it didn't take long for the *smell* of sex to intertwine
with the smoke and perfume. Marcia breathed in
deeply and smiled. She thought the aroma was a
fucking good smell!

She had been one of the first people to hit the
dancefloor, as the Necrowaltz was among her

favourite musical styles. Levene had initially danced with two different project males, but she had soon chosen to dance alone as neither of them had excited her wild sexual nature. Her predatory instincts involved a very selective type of pursuit and if anyone pursued her, she was usually turned off by their interest.

The nature of the masquerade ball being followed that evening usually had protocol that frowned upon verbal interaction between prospective partners, but when Levene tired of the two males that were drawn to her both received a whispered *fuck off* in their ears! On each occasion she had pulled the male toward her, as if she was going to caress his neck and then she had delivered her stinging rejections. The men were left to wander the floor on their own, annoyed and bemused at her teasing style of rejection.

After an hour on the dance-floor Marcia had found herself more interested in the sex on the conveyor – belt than trying to find a male who would match her sexual expectations. She was about to leave the floor and head for the bar when she was drawn to a man who danced alone underneath one of the lower conveyor-belt sections. At a distance he reminded her of Tavini. He was tall and another parallel was achieved because his long hair was black. She moved through the crowd in pursuit with her purple hair catching the lights – reflecting her presence. When she got close to her target the music changed. Levene wasn't familiar with the piece, but she was drawn into the strange ethereal sound nonetheless. Her quarry turned to face her and his dark eyes had a *piercing* quality to them. He knew the dance and as he pulled Levene into his arms, she was held in a very powerful grip that exacted a trance-like spell upon her. He honoured protocol and said nothing. Marcia was greatly intrigued by his presence and she wished that

he would speak. As the dance changed to a quicker
tempo, Levene was tightly pulled into the man's
chest. She still had no comprehension of the dance
steps that she was following, but she was distracted
by carnal thoughts. When the stranger had pulled her
to him, she had briefly felt the size of his manhood -
as his groin area had rammed tightly against her
stomach. She had visibly gulped in admiration and
she couldn't wait for him to penetrate her. She then
took the lead and roughly pulled the man away from
the dance-floor. In the shadows she thrust her
tongue into his mouth and then briefly spoke to him.

"You're going to *take* me now – back in my suite.
Fuck waiting, I know what I'm doing. Now preserve
your fucking silence if you must and follow me to
fuck me!"

The pair left the ballroom and Marcia pulled her
prey to the elevator. She was in a hurry now and didn't
need to flaunt herself any further, as she had secured
her chosen one! When the two of them stepped into
the elevator, Levene once again savagely kissed the
mysterious stranger, although on this second
occasion he tasted rather bitter and she broke off
quite quickly. She assumed that the harsh taste was
linked to the red wine that he had hastily finished off
when they were leaving the ballroom. Still a bitter-kiss
wouldn't stop her – not when she was with someone
who had a penis of such great size. His trousers
couldn't conceal his *immense* potential and Levene
eagerly anticipated her imminent penetration. She
rushed out of the lift doors, pulling her silent partner
towards her suite in desperate haste. The woman was
a little annoyed that he had still opted to maintain the
required masquerade silence, but all she had to do
was to think of that penis and he was forgiven! She
hurriedly unlocked her room and pulled her partner

through the doorway. She was determined to have sex on her terms and began with a list of instructions!

"I want you to *literally* rip me out of these fucking clothes. Then you'll roughly splay me across that bed, raise my arse in the air and fuck me *that way – up there* – for a starter! Don't worry if you hurt me. Pain is a pleasure of mine – I fucking love pain. Well, what are you waiting for? *Hurt* me!"

Levene's partner started to play sex *her way* – at least at the beginning. Her clothes were ripped apart by the man's large hands in a matter of seconds and then he threw the woman onto the bed. He added a novel twist to Marcia's instructions when he cut her on her back. Levene assumed that he was using a room key or some similar object. She realised that her cuts were *deep* when she felt blood trickling down her back. She was still impatient for penetration though and *shouted* another command to her lover.

"Now – damn you! Make my walls bleed! Just get in me, fuck me, fuck m-!"

Levene was cut short by the most powerful anal penetration that she had ever experienced. She had thought her *mystery partner* was still in the middle of the room not right on top of her! She had deliberately raised her arse on the bed and she had parted her cheeks to invite her penetration, but both factors had been tease – orientated to tempt her partner as he approached. Her partner had ideas of his own though, as Levene was beginning to find out!

The man inserted seven inches into Levene and then he rammed home the remaining six in one vicious thrust. She had an orgasm that reverberated through her whole frame, but she *prayed* that her partner now had his *full* shaft up her. She was unfortunate on that count!

He continued to grow *inside* her and panic spread through Marcia. She started to violently struggle,

wondering exactly *what* was on top of her! She gasped out a very anxious request.

"Please, please stop. Stop Sir please! This is torture – will you stop?"

Levene didn't exactly know why she used the word Sir, but at least it prompted a reply.

"No woman. I'm *fucking your new destiny*!"

"What the hell do you mean? What the fuck are you?"

"I am Klue – now be quiet bitch. It's time to enjoy the *breeding* season!"

With that line the *ultimate* horror of Klue's rape began. He kept ramming into Levene's anal passage, at an increasing speed that cut into her. Between every sixth or seventh stroke he would violently beat Marcia's back with one of his fists and pull back on her throat with the other, half asphyxiating her in the process. His breath now fully betrayed his vile identity and Marcia could feel the heat that accompanied it, with every sexual thrust. When Marcia had struggled to break free for a third time, Klue hit her so hard that she slumped to the bed like a ragdoll, with the energy knocked from her. As she endured the seemingly endless nature of her rape, the nightmare went a stage further.

Klue stopped for a brief moment, saying nothing. Then she felt something *tighten* inside her! To her horror, Marcia realised that Klue's penis had a form of *outgrowth* that locked his member into her anal flesh. She twisted to escape this new torture, but the spines of the outgrowth were like barbs once they were embedded and subsequently Levene was the victim of excruciating pain when she tried to break free.

When Klue was *locked* in place he briefly rested. Levene felt as though she had a column wrapped in scaffolding up her rectum and she just hoped for the ordeal to end. Then, just when Marcia thought things couldn't get any worse – they did!

She felt a faint tingling sensation around the entrance to her vagina. Levene could feel Klue's hands on her back and his penis was up deep inside her rectum, so initially she couldn't account for the movement. The woman was thinking that she must have imagined the sensation due to the shock that was pulsating through her, when the movement came again and something started to penetrate her *vaginal* passage! Klue started to rhythmically excite his *second* phallus and the second penis started to reach a state of erection! The horror of having one penis impaled up her arse while the second penis started to penetrate her vagina caused the woman to temporarily lose consciousness. When she recovered her senses some minutes later, both phalluses were fully erect and were simultaneously plunging into her. It was as though the first penis had been *docked* up her arse while Klue waited for his second phallus to become fully erect!

Now the devil had managed to get erect in the *conception* tunnel his speed threatened to snap Marcia's spine in two. He relaxed a little for the final thrust and then he shot his semen deep up Levene's vagina and simultaneously up her rectum. It took him just over a minute to finish ejaculating. More sperms had been released from the penis up Levene's vagina, but the one up her arse intermittently spat cum up her anal passage for a slightly longer duration.

The *beast* withdrew *twice* from his partner and after gently running a digit down her spine - he left.

A pair of firm hands woke the woman a couple of hours later. They belonged to a tall shaven-headed man in his late thirties. He wore a black suit. Levene had never seen him before. This man had a cold voice and no warmth lived in his eyes.

"We leave in a few minutes. You will change. You are going back to America. It is better that the *master's seed* is nurtured there."

The woman put on a warm coat in addition to some new clothing. The purple wig was left crumpled on the floor. She opened her room door and saw that the black-suited gentleman had two other men ready to escort Levene. Together the three of them walked the project woman out of the venue. They didn't meet any resistance – it was strangely quiet. The group then took a car to the banks of the Seine and the shaven-headed henchman spoke again.

"You are going to go on a short motor-launch journey and then you will make another car journey to the private jet that is waiting to fly you back to the States. If you try and escape we will cut your fucking womb out."

After this short destination breakdown, the four of them climbed into the motor-launch and started to follow the sinews of the Seine. A full-moon bathed Paris and to the ignorant the scene would have been impressive – three well attired gentlemen guarding a beautiful mature woman. The motor-launch broke through the moonlit surface and carried Klue's cargo out of Paris. The seeds had been sown.

ten

Before Levene had left for Paris she had instructed
security staff to give Feyer and Blackwell the same
comparative privileges that were given to the other
Avoider prisoners. The pair had initially been placed
in isolated confinement, but after Levene's *meeting*
with Feyer, they were subsequently housed with the
rest. It was Marcia's reward – her way of thanking
Feyer. She had authorised this new edict with a patent
hidden agenda, but Feyer was content to play along
because the *scent* of *freedom* was much more evident
in her new surroundings. Walking around the
recreation yard hardly compared with the Harz
Mountains, but it was a form of nirvana when
compared to the bondage that she had previously
experienced.

Feyer and Blackwell walked across the dusty yard.
Both of them feared the impending return of the
project *front-liners*, because they knew that
neurological alterations would eventually be
performed upon them. The waiting made things
worse in many ways and as a warm summer breeze
blew dust into their eyes, they gained a form of
solidarity by linking arms as they walked around their
prison. Some of their fellow Avoiders had already
been through the Prerogative Three ordeal and as
these individuals walked clumsily around the yard the

smiles of diminished cognisance gave them away.

Project security personnel had told the Avoiders about the implementation of the Leanworld Vision and each of them knew that the withdrawal of provision marked the *final* stage of the *genocide* of the wasted generations. Just over a third of the forty Avoiders walking across the yard were victims of Prerogative Three and Blackwell felt that he and Feyer should share some of their food with the wasted if they could. He saw this gesture as a type of moral-duty in a world that *didn't give a fuck*! He mentioned this to Feyer as they walked.

"We've got enough to share amongst a few of the wasted Feyer. We could always sneak some of our provisions out for the next exercise period. I can't stand watching them waste away. We eat well while they wither and fall. We've got to help a few of them."

"We'd just be prolonging the inevitable Blackwell. I like your fucking sentiment, but in a way it's kinder to let them be. Why should we prolong their stay in this shit-hole of a world? *Cruel to be kind* is a phrase that springs to mind here."

"By doing that we become as *stagnant* as the rest of society!"

Blackwell's choice of words involved an adjective that echoed through Feyer. She had called the world stagnant after she had aborted his child and for a moment guilt tore through her. Her next words reflected this emotion.

"Oh for fucks sake Blackwell. Ever the fucking martyr - aren't you? Death is their way out you know. If you had a sick animal, would you keep it alive?"

The couple would have argued further over morality and the starvation of the wasted, but a crashing sound interrupted their train of thought.

A large project-security vehicle had forced through

the perimeter wall of the prison and was speeding towards the Avoider prisoners. Feyer quickly looked at Blackwell. She thought that their last moment had arrived because the MC-Project seemed to favour *novel* ways of mass-execution!

The vehicle stopped a few metres from the prisoners and then a laser cannon was aimed at them. The project guards laughed and stood back, fully expecting to see another *massacre of the innocent.* Just as each *mentally – aware* Avoider expected the worst, the weapon was repositioned and started to blast the security guards behind them! In the ensuing chaos, a regulated voice sounded from the interior of the armour-plated vehicle.

"We can take seven - the first seven. We only have seconds!"

"Quick – the first seven!"

Feyer and Blackwell raced for the vehicle, as did the majority of the prisoners. Some of the *wasted* ran along with the others, enjoying the new game that they felt they were playing! As some Avoiders fought amongst themselves in the panic to make the *seven,* Feyer was roughly hauled into the vehicle. She looked around for Blackwell, but couldn't detect him in the flailing bodies that clambered to get inside. Then the woman was pushed down from the vehicle turret, into the darkness of the interior. She heard the voices of her rescuers and distinctly heard numbers four and five being called. Her heart cried out for Blackwell and sure enough he managed to claim the sixth allocation. His bloodied mouth smiled when he saw his *leader.*

After the seventh fortunate Avoider had been pushed down inside the vehicle, the three burly helpers jumped down below and the turret floor closed over. The vehicle then sped out of the prison yard with return fire blasting the armour-plated sides.

Feyer cradled her battered partner and for a short while the only audible sound was the rasping breath of the seven. A *familiar* voice then spoke to Feyer.

"Leaner than ever Feyer! It's good to see that you two are still in the land of the living."

The speaker was Dr Robertson, the Avoider who had tended Feyer after she had returned from the first Goslar massacre. She was surprised that he was still alive, thinking that he had been killed back in the Harz Mountains – when her pack had split from the main group. She expressed her surprise that *he* was still alive.

"It's great to see you're still with us too Dr Robertson! After my splinter-pack heard aerial bombardment in the vicinity where the main pack was located; we assumed that the worst had taken place. I don't think the rest of my crew made it though as Dean and I heard a rush of gunfire just before we were captured. How many of the others survived with you?"

"None. I had lagged behind the rest as we had started to climb higher and when the fighters attacked I was some distance behind them. The attack didn't last long and after the last plane had departed I raced ahead to see what I could do. Unfortunately a scene of devastation met my torchlight. Tangled flesh and bone lay in heaps. I couldn't find one *recognisable* Avoider and the power of the attack had been so *complete* that I didn't have any wounded to treat."

"So how did you get this far north on your own?"

"After the tragedy, my grief initially made me quite nonchalant as far as my own survival was concerned. I broke with the survival – criteria favoured by all Avoiders and started to walk alongside one of the northern roads. I was past caring you understand and when I realised that the occupants of a project security vehicle had seen me, I thought my time was up. It was the same vehicle that freed you and Blackwell – this one! It is one of the few that has been acquired by the Avoiders from the clutches of MC security! My expected enemy thus turned out to be my sanctuary – my guardian angel in effect!

"This group of Avoiders are born survivors Feyer. They've been active since the start and they are the antithesis of the laxity that was demonstrated by our old pack. In a few minutes all the new recruits will be blindfolded and no verbal account of our impending journey will be revealed to them. The scanning of Deadheads cost our olds pack everything and these Avoiders aren't going to make the same mistakes. We *minimise* location and route knowledge-sharing to preserve our security. We will discuss more tomorrow, but now your eyes have to be covered."

After the seven rescued Avoiders were blindfolded the vehicle left the outskirts of Hanover.

* * *

Later that day Jess Wheeler and most of the other project front-liners returned to the Hanover Designation. In Paris, Wheeler had been annoyed by Levene's disappearance, but this feeling turned to anger when he saw the wrecked compound. He ignored the body bags holding project security staff and concentrated on the damage done to his prison. His black knuckles were pale as he tightly gripped a machine gun. He was going to stop this laxity once and for all and he decided to take the retaliatory action immediately – before any reflective purpose could impede his vengeance.

Wheeler called for a *full*-assembly, ordering the entire project cohort and all the Avoider prisoners to the exercise yard. As the yard started to fill, one of Wheeler's security staff told him about the escape of the seven Avoiders and Jess turned a shade more *evil*

in an instant. He bellowed out his assemblage instructions, his eyes glinting in a portrait of pure-strain malevolence.

"Line up – damn you! We leave for a few fucking days and you security jerks have Avoiders snatched from right under your fucking noses! Someone's going to fucking well answer for your collective weaknesses this time. Right fat-man – come over here!"

Wheeler had selected one of his most experienced security staff members to come and stand beside him. He asked a question to the man, without engaging in eye contact.

"How long in the field employee 568? How many years project service have you seen?"

"Nine years Sir, nine glorious y-"

Wheeler's gun cut the man short. His blood splattered onto the uniform of the MC-Project Leader.

"Too fucking long in the tooth he was! He had lost the edge. Now remind me – it was seven who escaped wasn't it? That leaves six of you fuckers to go. First off, I'm going to lose those fucking *bliss slaves*. Hutchinson, waste the wasted – they just clutter up my fucking mind! Those fuckers don't count."

The project employee lined up the *wasted* against the wall and emptied his magazine. Blood started to colour large areas of the exercise yard. Wheeler then spoke again.

"You took too fucking long man! Sorry and all that shit, but I guess it's time to fucking kill you!"

The man looked for an instant as though he was going to turn his gun on Wheeler, but he hesitated at the critical moment and a shower of machine gun bullets ripped his face apart. Then Wheeler turned to the chief cook, salivating with the frenzy of killing.

"It's your turn now bitch!"

"Please spare me Sir. We are a project-family! We love our work."

"A family you say? How many exactly?"

"There are six of us sir. My husband, our four boys and myself. They are fine boys Sir: ready to serve the project."

"That's too many. You and your husband will decide which *five* of you are going to be shot. You've got one fucking minute to make your mind up."

The family openly wept, beside themselves with grief. They implored Wheeler to change his mind, but their leader had forged a decision straight from the *pit of hell* and it seemed unlikely that he would change it. The deadline passed and Jess Wheeler casually approached the family unit. The other MC-Project staff stood back leaving the *victims* in isolation. Jess announced his arrival.

"You can't make up your fucking minds can you? Never mind *Uncle Jess* is here to help out!"

As the family huddled together covering their eyes, Wheeler pointed his gun in their direction. Then at the last minute, he spun round and fired a burst of bullets into the *off-guard* project ranks. Five hit the floor dead, with blood pumping out of their gaping head wounds. Wheeler had *equalised* his deadly accuracy. He spoke coldly to the shocked assembly.

"Seven for seven! I guess we're done now, but if you ever repeat this form of weakness you will all wear your *eyes* around your neck! Be fucking warned!"

Wheeler walked away from the carnage, whilst the blood and corpses were cleared away. He whistled audibly as he left. The tune was a classical piece that celebrated the hot days of summer. It was an *upbeat* choice of music to whistle – the antithesis of tragedy!

Despite his *overshow* of confidence, Jess Wheeler was inwardly petrified. He knew that Klue would search him out that night and he feared that he would

110

have to answer for the escapees. He felt that Klue would see the escape as a weakness on his part – as though he was losing his *flawless* control. Sure enough the devil came on cue that night and spoke first.

"Messy Jess! In Paris my juvenile side informed me that a woman called Feyer was here. I fucking hope that she wasn't one of the seven escapees for your sake."

"I humble myself to you Klue. She was one of those who escaped, but she wouldn't have got out of this prison if I had remained. I've also lost Marcia Levene – you may as well know the full-scale of my weakness, my dishonour."

Klue was surprisingly calm.

"*I* secured Levene Mr Wheeler. As we speak, she is back in *your* country with my semen festering inside her. I have *raped* the world through Levene and spreading my coils around a disintegrating superpower.

"Losing Feyer was *slack* though Mr Wheeler – weak by your own admission. You see a woman like Feyer was *foretold*. She alone can damage my Empire. Only my other side can approach her in this region, because her *goodness stagnates my presence*! Do you see what damage you have done Jess Wheeler? You are to pay accordingly. It is time to gather my first *souvenir* – my first *privilege*."

Wheeler knew that pleas for mercy would hit deaf ears and he waited in the darkness like the *first time* – awaiting the satanic vengeance.

A searing white light burned into Jess Wheeler's left eye socket. After a split second this light retreated back into the darkness and Wheeler was left alone. He raced for the room lights, but something cluttered his night vision. When he eventually did turn the room lights on, he turned to look in the mirror and face the consequences of Klue's *judgement.* He swallowed hard and marvelled at the horrific cleanliness of the extraction. There was no blood, no gaping sore – just a bloodless hollow socket where his eye used to be. As he succumbed to the consequences of the savagery, he fell forward and *laughed.* The walls of the Avoider prison echoed with the manic sound and a bizarre irony hung over the scene – *the devil had stolen the evil eye!*

eleven

The new Avoider base was somewhere in Northern Germany. Feyer and Blackwell hadn't been told any location specifics pertaining to the exact whereabouts of the underground structure that they now resided in. Some fellow Avoiders told them that the building was one of a series of underground structures left over from the last century when *nuclear* unease still abounded. Germ and chemical warfare eventually became greater threats and the nuclear arsenals were left to corrode away. Decaying warheads leaked their radioactive poison into the metaphorical cess-pool that society had now become. The arteries of fallout provision were still dotted all over Europe and it didn't take long for these structures to attract those who were fleeing the MC-Project.

The Avoiders had to endure the squalor of these meagre living conditions, but they were quite safe in their underground isolation for the moment, because the project were primarily concerned with *colonising* unclaimed global regions. There was still talk though – darkened portents that anticipated *lethal* gassing or *parabrid* spore drops. This type of supposition always meant that sleep was tainted by nightmares.

After three days underground Feyer felt that she had swapped one prison for another. It wasn't as if she were chained to her bed like she had been previously, merely that existence seemed to be constructed by nihilism. The leaders of her new pack were *faceless* and no direct line of control seemed to exist. A bell would be rung three times a day to announce the provision of food for the Avoiders and up to a hundred would eat the food in a dimly-lit canteen area. Other than Blackwell and herself few Avoiders conversed, preferring the uniform silence of blanketed introversion. Life was comparatively shallow, even *boring* and the woman started to yearn for a bit of danger! Fear had effectively kept Feyer alive thus far and she was addicted to this negative impulse for that reason.

The one *saving grace* in the shelter involved a recreational area amidst the myriad of tunnels. This area had synthetic grassland and a real brook that was created from a series of underground springs. The Avoiders would visit this section in small groups or on their own, to contemplate the *better world* that had past them by. Feyer and Blackwell had first come across this area when they were finding their way around the shelter, but when she made her second visit she chose to go alone.

The woman skimmed stones across the surface of the brook, trying to hit a tall water reed that projected quite high out of the water. Eventually she tired of this pursuit though and as she looked at her reflection in the brook she remembered her LSE days and the years when London was still in *bloom*. A couple of Avoiders passed her by; exchanging a non- verbal greeting with their eyes and shortly afterwards Dr Robertson approached her. He, like Feyer was on his own. The man's voice cut into her world of contemplation.

"Hi Feyer. I guess you're finding this quiet life rather different to the pace of being continually pursued or the pain of being incarcerated by those project bastards?"

"Rhetorical questions don't beckon answers do they Dr Robertson? I'm just content to reflect on things at this moment in time. Life for us Avoiders seems to lurch from crisis to crisis. As soon as we feel that a quiet haven is reached, something shatters the peace. A big part of me is sick of fleeing, sick of our nomadic existence. Sometimes I wonder if the *wasted* or what's left of them are the lucky ones!"

"Very true – the *ignorance is bliss* cliché does fit the wasted extremely well. Have you lost all hope for the rest of us Feyer?"

"Yeah I guess I have now. In three months we are all going to be pitched into another bleak and miserable European winter. At the same time the project *fat cats* will lead their high life and slaughter us for sport! It's just a matter of time Dr Robertson – when they tighten the net all of us will be ground into non – existence."

Robertson pondered for a short moment, before replying to Feyer's pessimistic predictions. It wasn't the reply that she had been expecting.

"I agree with you – *ipso facto*. Have you ever thought of ending it all?"

"No – that would represent doing their dirty work for them. Many Avoiders must have taken the suicide option, but I'm fucked if I'm going to make things *easier* for the project!"

"Would that change, if you could take the MC-Project with you?"

"I don't follow you."

"If you had a way of wiping out the project in Europe and it meant being a martyr for morality, would you do it?"

"Of course I would, but aren't you being a bit melodramatic by engaging in this form of fictional supposition?"

"I wasn't utilising supposition, I was stating *a fact*!"

"You're talking in riddles here Dr Robertson! How can we cleanse Europe when we exist in a hovel like this?"

"You said *cleanse* Feyer – a word that has been semantically bastardised for a couple of centuries by global society. The only difference with our moral stance would involve us *literally* cleansing Europe – by destroying *all* the people in the said continent."

Feyer's mind was racing and after digesting the last remark, she returned to dwell on a significant word that Robertson had used shortly before his cleansing commentary.

"Hold on Dr Robertson. A while back you mentioned the word *fact* in relation to the European destruction of the project. How the hell can you have access to such means here?"

Robertson had been waiting to make his next speech to Feyer for some time now – long before the Harz pack separation. He had to be *sure* of his purpose and now the man felt he was. When the two of them had been reunited, everything seemed *predestined* in his eyes. He knew in his heart that this woman would be his *substitute* in the event of misfortune. He began.

"It is time to tell you a bit more about myself Feyer. I am a Doctor – that much is true. I majored in Medicine initially, but then my career developed in a more specialist direction, when the military recognised my affinity with chemical compositions. I was rushed through an accelerated second doctorate – but on this occasion I majored in *biological* warfare. I became involved with a group of *military chemists* who invented some of the most lethal Bio-Chem weapons ever created by man! When the project shut our research station down just over a decade ago my

colleagues were executed and the weapons were seized by the project – all but one batch that is! People assume that my bags are full of medical equipment and *most* of them are, but one black case was designed tough enough to *penetrate the orbit* because it is a container to house a Bio-Chem weapon. The black case has remained unobtrusive amongst my medical supplies. When I told you about the loss of the Harz pack, you must have wondered why I lagged behind my former colleagues when the main pack were climbing higher into the mountains. The reason was grasped tightly in my left hand. I was holding *that* case. Inside is one eight – inch glass cylinder that may look rather innocuous on first sightings. Appearances are deceptive here though because it is filled with twelve centilitres of vaporised *Plutura 26 B.* There are enough heavy metal elements and germ – based compounds in one small black case to wipe out *everyone* in Europe!"

Robertson paused for a brief moment and Feyer seized this opportunity to ask a question.

"So how long have you had this *lethal luggage* in your possession Dr Robertson?"

"Ever since the project ransacked our old headquarters! Effectively I've been a walking time-bomb and I suppose I must have led a relatively charmed life in that context. If my case had been destroyed during my time as a Harz-based Avoider, the cylinder would have done tremendous damage to the country in which it was detonated, but the full-scale of it's lethal capability wouldn't have been realised. You see, *Plutura 26 B* was devised as a *Continent-Buster,* but the nature of the malignant spore-base has to germinate in the right type of wind. Our lethal cocktail was specifically designed to take out Europe – not the buildings, just the people! We

researched how this deadly compound could advance
itself through hyper-speed mutant-germination. We
found that one type of wind accelerated the spread of
the germination ahead of all other wind types. This
wind involved a spiralling form of uplift and the
autumnal winds that blow to the west of Norway are
perfect for the destruction purpose. If the cylinder is
detonated when the spiral-winds are blowing, our
research showed that Europe would be devoid of
people in a shade under two hours – parts of Asia
would also fall under the malignant overspill. Are you
sure that you are ready to die?"

It only took a few seconds for Feyer to provide an
answer.

'I have no fear of death Dr Robertson – after what
I've been through it would be a blessing! On two
occasions recently I have felt the presence of
something so evil that the project's twisted nature
pales into insignificance in comparison. Initially I
encountered Klue through a *vision* and then the *beast*
paid me a visit. Before I met Klue, I thought that
angels and demons were folklore metaphors, but now
I know that the devil at least is a real entity. You know
me quite well Dr Robertson and I doubt if you would
question my sound of mind status. After my meeting
with *Satan*, I haven't got any realms of evil left to
confront. In a way this has strengthened my character
and *fired my resolve*. Europe is nothing but a
spawning ground for *his* kind of malevolence now
and the project merely accentuate things – creating a
combined dark force in the process. Europe died
years ago – shutting it down for good is just a *coup de
grâce*! Yes Robertson, I'm ready to die. In this sick
world I will embrace death as a *new dark virgin*!

A silence prevailed for over a minute and then
Robertson spoke again.

"Are you convinced that Klue's identity is *satanic*

and not conceived from your own world-weary-psyche?"

"I'm positive. I have mentally revisited the two occasions when I experienced his presence and I am now *certain* of the locale where my vision was based."

"Where was it?"

"A place in the Lofoten Islands – fittingly called Hell

"When I was a child residing in Norway, my family used to take me on holiday to the Lofoten Islands. I was only five or six then, but a few places have stayed in my memory. After the vision, I was initially too shocked to place the scene, but as the weeks went by I replaced the feeling of *déjà-vu* with firm recollections. The *Maelstrom* and *Hell* were two familiar ingredients to emerge from the vision and Klue's twisted juvenile side reaffirmed the landscape when it visited me. Klue has a beautiful lair you know – an aesthetic base from which to conceive the apocalypse!"

"Do you think that he has returned there now?"

"Only the wind and the seasons will know the answer to that question Robertson. I think that the fucker has a *chameleon* potential – it just melted into the darkness when it left my cell in Hanover and it *fused* through the waves in my Maelstrom vision. Don't you think that a *black irony* hangs over our European shutdown quest? The type of wind we need blows from Hell! It is conceivable that in order to wipe out Europe we will have to *confront* Klue!"

"I guess that if all the different factors come together that could transpire. Either way *death* stalks us. If you're willing to ride shotgun on this *suicide* mission I can tell you that I have got the route specifics – a conceived plan for reaching the area close to the Lofoten Islands. So far though, you are the only person to know of *Plutura 26 B.* We may need further cover in that context. Would you stake your life on Blackwell – or your *death* to be more precise?"

"I would."

Blackwell had effectively been included in the *mission* by a proxy-vote and Robertson added the name of Claire Hines by the same method. She was an adept survivalist who handled an Uzi as if it were second nature to her. Hines had the same tenacious spirit, as Feyer and that would mean that the pair would share great *kinship* or that only one of them would remain in the frame!

The pair continued to talk about their impending mission for some time. Their decision had been a cathartic experience for both of them and their sense of *release* was almost tangible. It was agreed that neither of them would approach the nominated *seconds* for a couple of days, so that they could fully digest the magnitude of what they were prepared to undertake.

* * *

A few hundred kilometres due south of the Avoider position the *form* tore through a dense forest. He had lost *her* scent when he had honoured the appointed place of *conception.* The *juvenile sentinel* had stayed to watch over the woman, but she hadn't resisted the temptations of a close – quarter meeting like Klue had instructed and her power had temporarily diminished as a result. After the conception he had planned to expunge her *powerful moral light* – not an easy task for an entity that was burnt by her presence. After the chaos that ensued during the breakout, she had flown from his snare. He stopped to stand and straighten to his full height. The glare of sunlight penetrated into the forest shade and the beast sensed that his realm of

ice was *aching* for the master's return. After a final surveillance he was gone, carried over the land by the route of the winds. Klue usually moved through people, but the *right* winds still took him *back*.

twelve

After Feyer had digested the implications surrounding the decision that she had entered into with Robertson, she remained convinced that *Plutura 26 B* held the answer to Europe's decadent slide. At first she had wondered whether the plan represented another form of *genocide* for the few moral people that remained alive, but the more she wrestled with their plan, the more she realised that it represented a mercy-killing. Robertson had told her that this particular form of germ-spore would render Europe a lifeless continent for at least two thousand years and it would become a *permanent* example of the futility surrounding this form of warfare. Maybe, just maybe the rest of the world might take heed from a *lifeless* continent.

When she had nominated Blackwell as her effective *second*, she had initially assumed that he would follow her lead as usual, but in the aftermath of her discussion with Robertson, doubts had set in. She had experienced a few misgivings surrounding the *finality* of their mission and she began to anticipate that he might not be immediately *sold-on* the idea of a *lifeless* Europe. Part of her wondered if she hadn't got too accustomed to his usual compliance with her wishes. She felt a form of guilt by the casualness that she had shown when she had made him a *suicide*

terrorist by assumptive proxy!

When she eventually broached the subject to Dean in the recreational section, she chose her words carefully. The couple were alone and a deceptive calm hung over the scene.

"Does your love for me hold any boundaries Dean?"

"No - none, why do you ask?"

"As you know, the two massacres I witnessed in Goslar sunk my spirit to an all-time-low. Our incarceration at the hands of the project made me feel even worse and it seemed that there were *no answers* to the hold that the project had over us. What I'm going to tell you about now involves something that is *worse* than the project, if you can comprehend something so evil! I have also discovered a *final* way of fighting back – a form of ultimate sacrifice for what's left of the *moral* world."

The woman held her breath for a moment and Blackwell chose not to break her flow with questions at this point. Feyer then detailed the evil surrounding Klue. It was painful for her when she revealed the details surrounding the self-abortion she had undertaken because Blackwell's seed had been destroyed by her own hands. She had felt impelled to tell Dean because Klue's juvenile side had used the extremities of her abortive action to try and *break* her. As she waited for the inevitable questions, she wasn't sure if her confession wouldn't act as a barrier to their future solidarity. After contemplating what Feyer had told him, Dean began his questions.

"I guess that *Feyer's way* didn't allow for the father to have any say, regarding the finality of your decision did it Feyer?"

"No. At the time it looked as though the Harz pack would remain together indefinitely or at least

until we were wiped out by the project. The no –
breeding policy was strictly enforced and I was an
Avoider who carried responsibilities."

"Exactly!"

"I can recognise your sarcasm Dean, but don't you
feel that a lot of *what-ifs* underpin your implied
condemnation? If we had *made love* like in the copse
as opposed to a *slam-bang* session, conception would
have been achieved from the warmest quarter. Then a
father has the right to know. If I had fallen pregnant
when my splinter-pack broke from the main group,
we could have wrestled things out and possibly raised
a child for a year or two, but too many *Herod's*
stalked Goslar in effect. Finally and most importantly,
if we were bringing a child into a comparatively stable
environment we could at least have something to offer
our offspring – a future. In our *sick* world all we can
offer is uncertainty and death. I still feel that I did the
right thing at the time. Can't you recognise that?"

"Only in part Feyer. I guess that I've *loved* you for
a longer period than your enhanced feelings toward
me. I worship the fucking ground you walk on – you
know. If a child had sprung out of our mutual
attraction for each other it would have endorsed *my*
love at least. You could have shared your *torment*
because in effect I shared your guilt!"

"So you agree then Dean, that bringing a child
into this world would be a fucking guilty action to
undertake?"

"Yeah, but undertaking an abortion on the quiet
also has a guilty *stigma* doesn't it?"

"Look, as far as the abortion is concerned I'm
sorry. If you place yourself in my position, you might
have done the same."

"That's a possibility I guess, but you'll never fully
know will you?"

The atmosphere noticeably cooled between the

pair and Feyer didn't quite know how to break the discomfort of her second *terminal* admission. It was Blackwell who eventually broke the awkward silence and carried their conversation further.

"What did you mean by final sacrifice?"

Feyer was initially stumped for words for once in her life.

"Well-er- if you get as low as-oh what the fuck, I don't know!"

"Come on Feyer spit it out! I've got nothing but time!"

After regaining her composure, the woman continued.

"Robertson isn't your average doctor Dean. He is skilled in germ warfare and in one of his cases he carries a spore that will wipe out the people in Europe for two thousand years! The contents of that case have to be activated in a type of autumnal wind that blows from a group of Islands to the west of Norway and from there it will spread a lethal pollution across the whole continent. We can't *win* Dean! We can't run forever, but at least this way we can take the bastards with us and hopefully *isolate* Satan in the process!"

"Sorry Feyer, first my chance of fatherhood is fucked up and then you recommend a form of *mass suicide* or *murder*! I'm going to need time to digest this – there aren't any quick answers regarding your *final sacrifice*! I'm going to think things over and if I see you again with a hail of Uzi bullets as my greeting card, you'll know that I've given Robertson's plan the thumbs down. I'll be seeing you."

As Blackwell walked away, Feyer was left to contemplate her situation. She had become so used to Dean Blackwell following her lead that she hadn't thought he would weigh up the merits of the decision to be taken. His last remark had stung her most, as

125

Blackwell had used the word i as one translation for Robertson's plan and that drew a parallel with the MC-Project. The woman kept playing the association over in her mind, but after an hour she remained convinced that *Plutura 26 B* was still a moral cull of all that was evil in Europe. Feyer felt sure that he would come round to her way of thinking – he had to!

When Feyer saw Robertson later that afternoon she told him about what had transpired between Blackwell and herself. The doctor became quite ashen and then spoke.

"What you said has greatly worried me Feyer. You see if Blackwell breaks the news of our intetions to anyone else here, we will be executed immediately. It is true that this group of Avoiders don't usually have a strict disciplinary code enforced upon them, but let us just pause for a moment and assess what our plan really represents to the non-committed. *The End* – that is your answer! If he breathes a word to the others we are as dead as the ranks of the *wasted.* When did he say he would get back to you with a decision?"

"He didn't commit a time or place."

"Well in that context we can make his mind up for him with this!"

Robertson showed Feyer a bone – handled knife to signify his intent.

"No! We should wait – we owe him that."

"When I broke the specifics behind our plan to Clare Hines, she *signed* up in a matter of seconds. Her exact words were *let's do it* and determination shone from her eyes!"

"Well I guess you think that a quick acceptance validates your choice as the correct one, but I still have faith in Dean nonetheless. He *will* commit after he has fully digested the implications of our plan. Hang fire with the knife. Dean Blackwell won't break

126

my trust in him."

"I'll give him one more day Feyer, but then if you haven't passed on his affirmative to me, I'll kill him."

Feyer slept uneasily that night. Since arriving in the Avoider base Blackwell had always slept with her They had been given some sleeping space at the end of one of the tunnels that ran through the base and although the living conditions were once again very Spartan, they were tolerable for a couple who had grown to love each other. Feyer missed Dean's strong arms around her. She understood that his absence was his way of coming to terms with the decision he had to make. The woman dreaded the implications surrounding Robertson's deadline because she wanted death to embrace them *simultaneously* – after they had successfully completed their mission. To Feyer, Blackwell represented the *perfect man to die with* and she didn't want Robertson's knife to alter this realisation.

The next day raced by and the deadline imposed by Robertson elapsed, but Blackwell still hadn't returned to the area where he and Feyer resided. She became worried that Robertson would find Dean before she did and so the woman headed for the recreation area where the pair had last met. The day was warm but overcast and this reflected Feyer's pessimism as she searched for Dean.

As Feyer passed under some willow trees a familiar voice spoke to her.

"Is that single – ticket journey still on offer *Ms genocide*?"

"Dean! Fucking great to hear you! Where the hell are you?"

"Up here."

The woman looked upwards and saw Blackwell perched in the branches of one of the willow trees. He jumped down and gathered her up in his arms. The couple then tore into each other's mouths as if it was the first time. After their kiss Feyer spoke first.

"Have you developed simian tendencies Dean?"

"No Feyer! *Climbing high* has been my way to contemplate since I was a kid. I can really focus on things if I escape this way. Up there I eventually saw the sense behind Robertson's plan. European society is so fucking *stained* now that there's no way back – there's no rescue plan to save the situation. That dream is dead as you and Robertson realised. I guess that my conscription took longer to develop, but after reflection, it is the *only* way left. The few moral individuals that would die initially made me averse to Robertson's plan, but now I've balanced this view by realising that the vast majority of people in this continent are our fucking enemies. In this context, the *cause* behind our fight is bigger than the last remnants of *decent* society. You were right, giving birth in this society would be like ushering a child into hell. I am in love with you and dying at your side will be an honour."

Feyer felt very relieved when Blackwell announced his decision and shortly after their meeting she managed to find Robertson. The woman stopped his pursuit before he had located his target and her relief was evident in her words.

"Your hunt is off Robertson. Dean is very much with us. It just took him a bit longer than the rest of us to reach that decision. I've just spoken with him."

Robertson had been primed for a confrontation, but Dean Blackwell would have effectively turned the tables on the older man if a fight had ensued. Robertson inwardly realised this factor and subsequently he was quite pleased at the nature of Blackwell's decision. It didn't stop him resuming his authoritative tone when all four group members met

later that evening. The appointed venue was Blackwell's sleeping quarters, set in the midst of the Avoider complex.

* * *

"This case effectively contains the *end* of Europe and I feel impelled to remind everyone that the nature of the contents stay with just the four of us. You will notice that the case has a combination lock attached to it. The relevant number is 6084277791 and it is impossible to get access to the contents without punching in these numbers on the electronic display panel. Please remember that this case and the contents by extension have been designed so durable that they can pierce the orbit! Once the case is opened, the glass cylinder is incredibly fragile. Please remember though that *Plutura 26 B* can only be effectively activated in the spiral winds."

Dean Blackwell asked Robertson a question.

"Do we just smash the cylinder on the floor Dr Robertson?"

"No. When you separate the cylinder from the case, you will notice a small detonation device underneath it. It is imperative that this is used because it launches the cylinder to a height of about ten metres before it explodes and shatters. If this is successfully completed the mutant spores will be released amongst the spiral undercurrent and the rest as they say will be history."

Robertson's *chosen three* surveyed the case interior realising the magnitude of what lay on the table in front of them. After each person had visually registered the contents, Robertson spoke again.

"Later today Feyer and I will be blindfolded for an audience with the Avoider leaders and the *route-finders* who will assist us in reaching Norway. This Avoider pack are a *dispersal-unit*. They don't function like other Avoider packs and serve to offer individuals or small groups a form of *scattered freedom* from where they can hide away and make a bid for survival on their own. Most of those who leave, return to their homeland and that will be our strategy. We will state that Feyer has family contacts in a pastoral area close to Oslo and we will subsequently ask the route-finders to research the safest way to get to Oslo. Their work is painstaking and it may take a few days before they have arrived upon a conclusion. We will never *see* the faces of those who are going to help us, but in a way I feel that is better. If Feyer and I weren't blindfolded we would offer *portraits* of our helpers in our main MC-Vault and the project bastards could generate more *wanted* posters. In many ways this will be the *hardest* part of our mission, because those who are helping us will inevitably become innocent victims of the *final solution* that we are undertaking. This cruel irony shouldn't deter us from our purpose though. People like the brave souls who are helping us are so *rare* that their collective loss is negligible when we kiss goodbye to Europe."

Robertson's words were in Feyer's mind when her blindfold was fitted over her eyes a few hours later. A subordinate of the dispersal-base leaders undertook this task and then she and Robertson were led to their appointment.

The atmosphere at the meeting was very supportive. There weren't any austere voices or egocentric displays from those willing to help them and collective warmth exuded from the three people that were in charge of the dispersal base. Feyer obviously felt sorrow for the three as Robertson had expected she might do, but if anything this strengthened her resolve for the task ahead of the Avoiders. The closing address of the main speaker was almost *prophetic* in terms of relevance.

"Our route-mapping research will take a week to ten days and you should be ready to leave by mid-August in that context. Unusual weather conditions have been apparent in your chosen area of retreat this summer, but this temporary aberration will probably have returned to the proverbial mild climate synonymous with Norway, by the time you three leave us. We wish you good fortune in your escape and we hope that you can find peace. It is our collective opinion that *all* of us have but a short time left – enjoy that time."

Feyer and Robertson thanked their helpers and were then led back to Robertson's sleeping quarters. The pair briefly talked about the meeting and then they individually went to locate Blackwell and Hines. Dean was pleased to see his partner but Hines was initially rather *cold* with Robertson as the woman felt that *she* should have gone to the meeting. A form of jealousy was starting to build in her and that didn't bode well for a mission that needed to be underpinned by mutual respect if it was going to be successful.

The subsequent days were very enjoyable for Blackwell and Feyer as each respective day was entered into as though it were the last. The pair lost count of how many times they made love whilst they waited for the route-masters to reach a conclusion and those days effectively represented some of the happiest that both of them could remember. On the tenth day the Leaders summoned Robertson and afterwards he reported back to the other three.

"The route-masters have done their work and we go tonight folks! A freight train has undertaken a night journey to Oslo for the last four consecutive nights. The specific nature of the freight is unknown because each truck is covered with a loose-canvas hauling. The train doesn't stop at stations, but it refuels just south of here. That is the location where we will board the train and hide amongst the freight. We will be in Norway in a shade over twenty hours. The weather is still very weird for this time of year and so all of us will have to wear our warmest clothing."

After Robertson had spoken, everyone made ready for the overnight journey and adrenalin shot-through their veins as they prepared. When the departure time drew near they were blindfolded for the last time and driven to the perimeter of the refuelling post. Upon arrival they fondly embraced the *dispersal* helpers and then when the vehicle drove away, they lay in wait for the freight train. They occupied a lofty vantage point on a small bridge above the rail track and their conceived plan involved them jumping into the freight trucks when the freight train pulled away from the refuelling post.

The four of them lay on the bridge in uniform silence until the train arrived. They said nothing for fear of attracting the attention of the personnel who fed the one-kilometre long train with diesel ready for the long-haul ahead. When they were done. The powerful engine belched a release of pressure and then it slowly started to pull away. The four of them waited for the first five trucks to pass under them and then Blackwell and Feyer made their leap. Robertson and Hines quickly followed suit, landing in different trucks.

As soon as Feyer contacted the light canvas covering, she fell inside the truck and received the shock of her life. An overpowering *stench* caused her to vomit within a matter of seconds and her left arm penetrated something glutinous. She screamed out for Blackwell to switch on his torch and when he did, a sight of death-camp proportions met their eyes! The

contents of the freight train involved the rotting
corpses of the *wasted*! Feyer's left arm had passed
clean through the stomach of one such corpse and
she screamed at the horror pertaining to their
situation. Blackwell then retched before joining Feyer
in his own expression of disgust. Their fellow
passengers in the freight truck looked like a scene
from a zombie horror-flick and it was going to be a
very long twenty hours!

The pair had discovered a new all time low point
and then lightening started to cut forks into the
evening sky to make matters worse still. The Avoiders
had been informed about the untypical weather that
was causing havoc across Europe, but they had *never*
witnessed an electrical storm of such magnitude.

As the train tore through the night the lightning
intensified and started to make contact with the
ground on occasions. A lurid glare was given off as an
electrical *battleground* ensued and pallid portraits of
the dead flickered inside the freight trucks with each
successive strike. Feyer lay slumped on the corpses of
the *wasted* and directly opposite her a decomposing
mother and daughter became an image that kept
dominating the woman's visual register. Eventually
the couple proved too traumatic a portrait and Feyer
flung her coat over the faces of the pair of them.

The long journey that the freight train was
undertaking initially ran eastwards across Europe,
before a sharp northward deviation would be
undertaken. After speeding through several European
countries, Norway would eventually be reached by
following a westward direction. Blackwell and Feyer
had been rendered silent bar their screams when they
had landed amidst the corpses, but the woman
eventually managed to speak to her partner.

"Hour after hour with these fellow passengers is

going to be a new kind of hell Dean! I think I'm clean out of vomit!"

"Yeah! Robertson reckoned that this journey will involve a twenty-hour duration – how the fuck are we going to survive the stench for that long?"

"One consolation is that Robertson was wrong Dean. He kept quoting the journey time to Oslo! That city is down in southern Norway- hundreds of kilometres too far south! I expect that this fucking train will refuel again in northern Norway. We'll make our departure at that point."

"Where do you think that the train will refuel then?"

"*Bodo* or somewhere close."

Feyer had rightly anticipated Bodo to be a refuelling stage. Her Norwegian roots had come into play in her deduction, because she knew that the long haul south would mean that the train would have to stop somewhere in the north for refuelling purposes. Her prediction *would* come to fruition, but not before the electrical storm became more *deadly* in terms of effect.

Suddenly the forked lightning took a vicious turn for the worst. The power of the bolts seemed to increase and then isolated freight trucks were hit. Initially these trucks were some way down the line from Feyer's truck, then the bolts started to edge their way gradually closer. Most of the freight trucks that had been hit had burst into flames upon impact and as the lightening grew closer still, Feyer hoped that the apparent randomness of the strikes would spare their truck. Robertson and Hines were four trucks behind them and the *Plutura 26 B* case was still in their hands. Feyer and Blackwell peered over the top of their truck and saw some movement in Robertson's truck – when one particularly violent strike blasted the contents of the truck adjacent to his! Robertson

lost his calm and started to panic. In desperation he began to climb across the line of freight trucks in the direction of their truck. The lightening spat evil forks all around him and eventually the inevitable happened. A double-blast hit the man with one bolt scorching him with a severe burns-ratio and the next made sure – stopping his heart for good as he valiantly *clawed* his way to Feyer's truck. Robertson then fell from the train – brave but very much *dead*!

Hines sobbed as she witnessed the destruction of the man she loved. She tightly pulled the *case* to her breast. Her eyes now *hated* with the kiss of vengeance.

After the loss of Robertson, the storm seemed to subside quite quickly. In their respective trucks the Avoiders sunk lower amongst the decomposing corpses, saying nothing but fearing everything. It was as though *nature* had suddenly become *malevolent* – being controlled by the evil that they aimed to suppress.

Klue had enjoyed *his* storm, even though he had missed his *main* target. He would wait.

thirteen

The *disposal* train raced on across Europe, tearing through Poland at a speed of just under two hundred kilometres an hour. Feyer had pulled her black scarf over her face as the stench of the decomposing flesh around her had become unbearable. Blackwell cradled her in his arms, saying nothing but longing for the destination where the three of them could disembark. Meanwhile Hines was still coming to terms with Robertson's loss. The two of them had been very close for over a year and she found it hard to fully comprehend life without him. In this context, the case that she clutched so tightly had a dual – symbolism – Robertson and the *end*. Hines had raised herself on top of the festering corpses and from her lofty position she stared out at Europe with hostility in her eyes.

When the train reached *Kaumas* in Lithuania it stopped at a goods yard. The Avoiders were there to take on more fuel, but unfortunately the horror story that they were experiencing was going to take another turn for the worst!

As the trucks started to slowly pass underneath the freight-loader the Avoiders had a brief moment of contemplation. Years before grain or other produce would have filled each freight truck, but now the *feeder units* had been widened to drop *more* corpses into them! When the bodies were spat out of the

feeder unit, some split apart due to the rotting nature of the flesh. The Avoiders waited to receive the shower of corpses. They had to *play dead* because if they shifted their movements would probably have been noticed by the loaders above them. They were subsequently powerless to do anything but wait for the rotting flesh to rain down on them.

More corpses were deposited into the freight truck in front of Feyer's truck and the sound that the bodies made when they dropped through the canvas covering inspired further revulsion. As corpse landed on corpse a series of dull thuds could be heard and a second sound accompanied the thudding. It was akin to the sound fruit pulp made when it was compacted in a tight area. This second sound was in actuality the noise that the rotting bodies made as they *split* on impact. The smell generated by the drop perfectly married the macabre visual spectacle and Hines could detect the potent presence four trucks down the line. She watched the corpses spew down ahead of her and prepared herself for the deluge!

The bodies started to rain down on Feyer's truck and she and Blackwell remained as still as the dead around them. Corpse after corpse dropped through the centre – gap in the flimsy canvas covering and several split their grisly contents over the pair of Avoiders. The truck had three metres in depth to fill until it was brim-full and Feyer prayed that a *full-load* wasn't planned; otherwise she and Blackwell could be asphyxiated by a tide of decomposing humanity!

Fortune was with the pair for once as the deposit stopped after a metre of depth had been delivered from the feeder chute. This still represented a compacted weight of some bulk and Feyer fought for oxygen as the rotting flesh obstructed her airways. She would have suffocated under the corpses if

Blackwell's strong arms hadn't been there to pull her up.

When the woman did manage to *surface* she gasped for air in rasping breaths. Both of them *stank* of decaying flesh. She regained her senses and then quietly spoke to Blackwell in a muted voice - for fear of being heard by the feeder chute workers who were now filling the adjacent truck.

"Why the fuck is this train taking on *more* rotting human freight Dean? The *wasted* were just left to rot where they died before."

"If what we've heard and seen represents the full-truth Feyer, I guess that Europe is littered with *millions* of *wasted* corpses right now. The sheer *volume* of the dead will demand a form of mass disposal. We landed on rotting human corpses and my guess is that they are going to jam-pack these trucks all the way to Oslo. I'm fucking glad that we jumped train before then!"

"What you say makes sense Dean. I guess in that context it does look as though Oslo is one of their dumping sights. Fuck humanity – I can't wait to end it!"

The couple had correctly diagnosed the function of the freight train in relation to the European genocide. Their train was one of fifty bound on a course for Oslo. Each carried the same grisly contents and millions of corpses were destined for the disposal pyres just north of Oslo. In effect the capital of Norway had turned into Europe's burial ground. The train continued through Latvia and Estonia before it briefly ventured through the Russian federation. In Finland the freight trucks were filled to the maximum level and each of the three Avoiders made it to the top again without being detected.

Once the train had entered the *midnight sun* countries, it slowed down quite substantially. The bodies of the *wasted* were piled high on each freight truck and a dark kind existed with the symmetrical pyramids of corpses overriding each respective truck. The train started to snake around the Scandinavian countries that bordered the Barents Sea and eventually it arrived in Norway. Feyer was now in a state of full alert because she knew that a refuelling stop must be imminent. The terminal destination of Oslo was hundreds of kilometres too far south and she reaffirmed to Dean that they must *jump train* at the next stop. She had hoped that the train would stop at Bodo, but when it came to a halt ten kilometres to the north of that particular destination she turned to Blackwell and recommended a disembarkation.

"Yo Dean it's time to leave this coffin carrier. Who's going down the line to tell Hines?"

"My shout Feyer. Jump off the left side and we'll do the same. Hit the bushes when you land. Love you!"

After Dean Blackwell had opted to be the one that told Hines, he started to crawl along the ridges of the freight trucks to inform Hines of their decision. He found her trembling. Her eyes were wild and her face was a portrait of vengeance. Blackwell spoke in a whisper because several project personnel were close by monitoring the refuelling of the powerful engine.

"Disembarkation time Claire!"

"Robertson quoted Oslo to me Blackwell. I stay *fixed.*"

"The *spiral winds* blow from the northwest. Oslo is far too southern for our purpose. Come on woman, hand me the case."

"Leave me. The pair of you can find a form of sanctuary in Norway – at least for a while."

"No, I'm not moving a inch without that fucking case!"

139

"*He* was *my* leader you know I *loved* him! He was my fucking inspiration. I can't move on the orders of others. Leave me and give me a little peace to reflect on my loss."

Things definitely weren't going to plan. It was obvious that Hines was having great problems coming to terms with the loss of Robertson and Blackwell realised that she had to be shocked back to her senses. He took hold of the pistol that he had in his combat belt and he pointed it directly at the woman. He managed to maintain the whispered nature of his oral delivery, but his eyes now bore a new savagery that meant he wouldn't be challenged when he made *demands*.

"Look woman! Wake the fuck up! If I have to give you a *third* eye with this gun, I fucking will! Those fuckers behind me will have refuelled this train soon and Feyer's waiting. I'll give you ten seconds to decide whether you're coming with us or whether you're going to join Robertson now!"

Claire Hines didn't need ten seconds. She flung Blackwell the case and scowled at him before asking one question as she prepared to disembark.

"Which side to your ladylove Blackwell?"

Her words stung with sarcasm and Dean echoed her tone in his reply.

"Over the left-side to join my Queen of women Hines. Go and serve her!"

After a second evil stare, Hines made her jump-off, followed by Blackwell shortly afterwards.

The Avoiders all jumped eventually and as the train passed them by they knew in their hearts that they had seen the *last* of the *wasted*. Tavini's Leanworld Vision became his legacy and the trains of the dead became the final signifier of his evil presence.

After the last freight truck had passed, the three

Avoiders walked alongside the rail track. Feyer told the others that they needed to get to Bodo before the *full* glare of daylight dawned. She planned for Blackwell and Hines to lie low for a few days when they got there, whilst she assessed how much of old Norway had been preserved in Bodo. If the harbour still abounded with the fishing vessels that it was synonymous with during her childhood days, then the three of them could reach the Lofoten Islands by stealing one of the boats. So much depended on whether the *scars* of the MC-Project had penetrated that far north. Both she and Robertson had felt that the land above the Artic Circle might be comparatively *unscathed* but that was before they had experienced the trains of rotting corpses! The woman smelt her clothing and bile came into her throat instantly. She suggested to the others that such an aroma would arouse suspicion in anyone who encountered them and she was also worried that they ran the risk of contracting serious diseases from their close proximity to the corpses. She voiced her concerns.

"We've got to remove the fetid smell on our clothes folks. Part of me thinks that we ought to go back and kill the freight-loaders for their uniforms, but that would alert every project fucker north of Oslo and so I guess we're stuck in what we're wearing for the time being. Oh and if either of you have got any pills to counteract our exposure to rotting flesh it would be a bonus!"

Both Blackwell and Hines shook their heads and Feyer injected a bit of black humour in an attempt to lighten their mood.

"Never mind, it was a rather ironic request anyway – pills to keep us alive long enough to commit suicide! What a weird fucking world!"

She then asked the others to look out for a water source so that they could attempt to clean themselves up. As the daylight slowly intensified, Hines spotted a river glistening in the distance. It was the first time she had *spoken* to her fellow Avoiders since leaving the train an hour ago.

"I can see a river – about a kilometre away in a north-west direction. Here you are woman use these."

Hines passed Feyer her field-binoculars. Her tone was still cold with the other two, but she felt good about being the first person to spot bathing water. In a small way it was a semi-triumph for her and the others were drawn closer to her for an instant.

The three of them deviated from the banks of the railway track and headed for the distant river. Blackwell tightly grasped the case of *Plutura 26 B* and as he walked on the springy grass, he whistled an annoyingly cheerful tune given their circumstances. The *whistler's* clothes were caked in rotting flesh and he carried the *end of Europe* in his hands! Despite these two factors he suddenly felt a strange kind of elation! Europe was now a social quagmire and holding the power to shut this pitiful continent down lightened his spirit for a while. What he held made him the most powerful *man* in Europe at that moment in time! He laughed out loud at his realisation and Hines snapped at him – wanting to know what could possibly be funny in the context that they found themselves!

"What the hell have you got to fucking laugh about Dean? Humour died years ago!"

"Maybe, but don't you two get just a small buzz when you think of our suicide mission? Here – catch!"

Blackwell had thrown the case up in the air and Feyer angrily caught it. She was furious at his infantile behaviour, temporarily forgetting that the

142

case could withstand orbit penetration!

"What the fuck are you up to Dean. Remember that cylinder can only be properly activated in the spiral winds. We're fucked well and truly if you break it now!"

An unusual sound interrupted the pair – Hines was laughing! After contorting with her laughter, the woman spoke to the pair with a *smile* on her face.

"Lighten up Feyer! You sprung up for that case as if it was made of china! Come on girl you've got to see the funny side. I mean that case is an *orbit-buster*. He set you up a treat really didn't he?"

Feyer did eventually manage to see the humour in what Blackwell had done and her face creased into a smile too. There was precious little to smile about in their world and so she started to enjoy the rarity of what was taking place. When the trio reached the banks of the river, the levity continued and Dean took the lead again.

"Right girls, I'm Dean Blackwell modelling the latest outfit in my *rotting-flesh* line and now I'm going to discard my *fall* collection!"

After extending a cheeky grin to the women, Blackwell started to peel off his clothing. Soon he was naked, striding into the shallows with his foul smelling clothes in his hands. When he was up to his waste in water, he looked back and issued a challenge to his fellow Avoiders.

"Come on girls it's your turn now – I hope that you're not too modest to rise to a challenge!"

Feyer verbally sparred back as she started to peel out of her clothing.

"Sure we'll rise to your challenge, but in that cold looking water I reckon that *one* part of you won't be rising!"

Feyer entered the water and proceeded to splash

Blackwell. The pair then beckoned Hines to come
and join them. She was still fully clothed and had a
vulnerable look about her. Feyer thought about the
woman's appearance for a moment and then briefly
reflected on the key events of the last twenty - four
hours. Hines was probably *mourning* the loss of
Robertson and seeing another *couple* tease each other
in the water must have brought back memories for
her. It was easy to suppress death in their world of
savagery – that is unless your *closest* soul-mate was
killed. Feyer modified her voice accordingly and
spoke to Claire in a much softer tone than before.

"Come on in Claire – join us! You've got to wash
the filth from the clothes you know. He was a good
man and we'll all rejoin him in a matter of weeks. It's
just a temporary parting you know. Come and
celebrate the *last of life* in the water. Do as we do and
live for the last moments."

The softer side of Feyer managed to turn Hines
away from her negative reflections. It was true that
the couple splashing in front of her had initially
reminded her of the brief intimate liaison that she and
Robertson had shared, but there had been a lot of
sense in Feyer's intuitive words nonetheless. She
slowly started to shed her clothes and when she was
naked her lithe frame approached the water.

When she reached the couple all three of them
formed as they stood in the water. They said nothing
initially but bowed their heads in unison as they
discovered a *bonded* solidarity. Each of them had
placed their soiled clothes in the shallower water and
subsequently their hands were now free. The triad
started to gently massage each other's shoulder
blades and they simultaneously started to raise their
heads. A strange kind of synchronisation governed
their actions, almost as if they were acting beyond
themselves – directed by the hands of a cohesive

unifying force. After some minutes, it was Hines that spoke first.

"Robertson told me about Klue Feyer. He said that our mission involved a double-hit to wipe out the project in Europe and to kill or stall the devil."

"He was correct Claire. From the little I know I doubt if Klue can be killed. I get the impression that he moves through humans – especially their frailties. After we've detonated *Plutura 26 B*, he won't have anyone left to feed through though. In effect we will make the fucker dormant."

"Tell me about Hell Feyer."

"It's where we are heading! No fire or rebel angels-just a derelict settlement at the southern tip of Moskenesoya. It's *usually* warm and mild at this time of year, but I'm not sure that we will find it that way when we locate it. The storm last night had evil portents written all over it and the dispersal Avoiders had told Robertson that the weather over Norway had turned a shade weird for this time of year. It's as though Klue is shielding his lair from the *unwanted* and I just hope that all three of us can make it through. The spiral winds will start blowing in a couple of weeks and it's almost as if the devil knows our purpose! If that's true, taking out Robertson was our closest call yet, but we'll pay the bastard back when we visit him."

Without knowing it Feyer had been quite intuitive with regard to Klue's *defence* strategy. The *beast* only feared Feyer out of the three Avoiders. She seemed to be following a *predestined* path and her presence *stung* him if he looked too long at her. Since the dawn of time *his* legions had always feared a prophesised female figure that spat *fire at their ice*. The woman was reputed to bring with her flaws to mark her strength and thus she could be vanquished. It was predicted that the satanic legions *could* harm those who denied the master and thus *this* Satan would have a strong reliance on his *mortal* defenders, if Feyer proved to be the spirit of prophecy. Not all the satanic prophecies were incarnated by the figure of Feyer, but a central warning did ring true. It was stated that a woman *that carried the future by name* could block Klue's vision. An ancient Norse translation of the word Feyer implied that a person christened with that name was a *seer* and thus one salient prophecy was on the side of the Avoiders! The woman was slowly starting to *realise* the ethereal form of inner-strength that singled her out from the rest – she was rising to the fight.

Klue could *smell* the woman's moral spirit drawing nearer to his lair. He had withdrawn to his Lofoten sanctuary to prepare for the *Final Encounter* with her – if she made it that far! He had *summoned* Wheeler and his security forces to his island in readiness for a confrontation. Klue now sensed that Wheeler's men had started to lose faith in their one-eyed leader. The man who was once the most feared security presence in the western world now stooped a little and his face was drawn by the spectre of perpetual torture. He seldom conversed with his project subordinates and they knew nothing of the devil's *motivating* presence. If he did talk to his men, it was to bark an order or deliver a stinging threat and only Marco Sant remained loyal to the course that Wheeler was following. When Klue had ordered Wheeler to bring his security cohort to Moskenesoya, Jess hadn't given *any* reason for the latest geographical shift and his troops became even more disillusioned. The decadent high-living that the project staff had previously experienced was now redundant and was replaced by the uncertainty associated with playing the tune for a psychotic leader!

Before the cohort left for the Lofoten Islands, a mutiny took place and a significant number of security staff fled to isolated parts of Northern Germany. In many ways *the party was over* and when two deserters were caught, Wheeler was *ruthless* in his implementation of justice once again. Both men were hung by their ankles and repeatedly cut across vulnerable areas of their bodies until they bled to death. Wheeler had announced the deaths to his men as *the last fucking warning* and when the remnants of the security division boarded the helicopters to take them to Moskenesoya, project morale was at an all-time low.

* * *

One of the helicopters flew high above the heads of the bathing Avoiders and all three of them registered the unmistakable sound of the craft. They looked at each other, thinking the same thought. The project choppers were flying in the direction of the Lofoten Islands and Feyer felt that this represented a *massing* of the enemy! She sensed the work of Klue once again.

The Avoiders dried out their clothing and then proceeded to walk the remainder of the journey to Bodo. Although it was later in the day than their first journey estimations had predicted, they didn't encounter anyone as they walked beside the rail track. An eerie silence was in the air when they reached the outskirts of the town. The sound of the disposal trains as they sped past occasionally broke the monotony of the cloying blanket of silence, but initially humans were totally absent from the streets of Bodo. This factor instilled fear into the Avoiders. The three of them were now exhausted from their gruelling journey and they decided to break for the night before venturing further into Bodo.

147

Klue would send his storms again that night and as he soiled nature with malevolence, his *handmaiden* sunk her teeth into his fetid phallus. The beast *snarled* when he came and the air became pungent around him. His diseased semen seeped into the earth and he turned his thoughts to the *satanic* triplets developing in Levene's womb. The beast then bit down on his handmaiden and she returned a demure smile for receiving his pain – it was the benediction that she had desired and after receiving it, she drifted into a contented sleep at the feet of her master.

fourteen

The three Avoiders had slept in the grounds of a deserted, large residence in the outskirts of Bodo and Feyer was the first to wake. She gently woke her two companions and then laid out the plan of action for the impending day.

"We ought to assess our surroundings thoroughly today guys and undertake a reconnaissance of the centre of Bodo. We can get the lowdown on why it's so fucking silent here and where all the citizens of Bodo have gone. We're bound to find *some* people in the centre of the town. When we do encounter others, let me converse. They'll speak Norwegian – the language that I was raised in."

Whilst the three Avoiders still looked rather bedraggled, they didn't look as noticeable as they had done, before they had washed the rotting flesh from their clothes! When they got close to the centre of the town they sighted an elderly couple. Feyer made her move, whilst the others stood back not wishing to frighten the couple with their added presence.

Feyer smiled at the couple as she approached them, hoping that this universal gesture would allay any fear that they may have had for strangers. When she got closer to the pair, the old man stood protectively in front of his partner. She then spoke in a tone that was reassuringly warm and friendly.

Her expression broke their fears down and the

three of them conversed for a few minutes. Feyer then thanked the couple before making her way back to Hines and Blackwell. Her face had suddenly become quite ashen. She divulged what she had learnt to the others.

"Bodo was the scene of *another* project atrocity six months ago. Northern Norway had been comparatively unscathed until then, according to those old folks. Oslo, Bergen and other southern cities had been hit years ago with the mandatory Prerogative Three edict, but life on the western coastal fringes had managed to retain the old ways in the main. The couple stated that they had been aware of the radical changes that the MC-Project had made around the world, but they had started to feel *safe* in their backwater isolation. Then the project had moved into the north-west and a killing-spree had been entered into. The troops didn't bother with Prerogative Three – they just disembarked from their gunships and started shooting the citizens of Bodo. *Everyone* was executed, save the very old. The *fucking bastards* even shot sleeping infants! After three days the shooting stopped, but the couple said that the massacre had been *total* as far as they knew."

"Where does that leave us – with regard to getting to the Lofoten Islands?"

"It shouldn't be a radical problem Dean. They said that project security squads haven't been back since the massacre and the harbour is still packed with the boats of countless dead fishermen. We can take our pick."

Hines then asked a question.

"When do you think we should make our move?"

"Not for a couple of weeks. The spiral winds won't start blowing until September. We may as well lie low in this ghost town until then. Bodo is a haven when compared to the uncertainties that await us in

Moskenesoya – the island where *Hell* is located."

The three Avoiders continued to plan their impending journey and Blackwell was designated to select the most suitable vessel for their passage. He had some maritime navigation experience and he quite liked the idea of being in charge – for a change! In the next few days they occasionally saw some more elderly people, but the place had the atmosphere of a morgue – it was restful but deathly silent. No bird song could be heard and Bodo had the atmosphere of a second *Auschwitz*.

After finding out that Bodo was nearly deserted the Avoiders chose a very elegant residence to occupy. It had many rooms with an ornate staircase being just one of it's many aesthetic features. The residence was in close proximity to the harbour.

That evening Feyer had plans to temporarily lighten the gloom that enshrouded Bodo. It had been *another* oppressive day and she felt that the onus was on her as leader, to find a form of respite from the tragic discoveries that frequently came their way. When Blackwell and Hines were sorting out an evening meal from tinned foods that they had scavenged in Bodo, Feyer quietly made her way down to the cellar. She had anticipated that the property they had *claimed* would have some wine racks down in the cellar. As she walked down the cellar steps she hoped that her deduction wouldn't be a case of *wishful thinking*!

The woman's face lit up when she saw a wine rack containing about fifty bottles! After briefly looking over the selection, she walked back up the stairs clutching the finest bottles of champagne and claret that she had ever seen. She burst into the kitchen with the enthusiasm of a teenager on her first sleepover!

"Yo – it's party time guys – time to liven up this

gloom-tomb!"

She threw a bottle of champagne to her fellow Avoiders and after securing a corkscrew she proceeded to gulp down large mouthfuls of claret.

Hines smiled and was most complimentary to Feyer. This was a far cry from the days before the *infamous* train journey – when the pair had been openly hostile toward each other.

"Cool Feyer – a real bonus! I guess I sussed you wrong earlier you know. Sorry *pack-leader*. Yeah we'll sure make it a fucking booze session to remember. Time to party like it's the last time – I guess it could well be!"

Hines had uttered her last line with an impish smile on her face. She had seen the *dark humour* attached to her choice of words and then the other two saw the linguistic irony. All three of them proceeded to laugh in a good-natured communion.

The first batch of alcohol was drunk extremely quickly, proving a welcome temporary antidote to the horrors that they had experienced. When the first bottles were emptied, Blackwell went down to the cellar to retrieve some more. That gave Feyer time to speak to Claire. She was about to extend a very unusual offer to her fellow female Avoider.

"Do you fancy having Dean tonight Claire?"

Hines nearly fell off her kitchen bar – stool in surprise, before she managed to respond to Feyer.

"You what! He's yours. He, he-"

Feyer cut-in.

"It's fine Claire. I've seen you looking at Dean – that's natural cos he's a good-looking guy. If we look at things rationally for a second Claire – we'll all be dead in a matter of weeks one way or another. *Possessions* don't count for anything now. We've just got to live for the fucking day. I sure don't mind *sharing* and I reckon Dean would get off over fucking someone else when we're so *close to the wire*!"

With that remark Feyer left Claire to contemplate being fucked by someone that she had only masturbated about until that night. She became wet with excitement.

In the cellar Feyer got straight to the point as always.

"Hey Dean. Do you feel like fucking Claire – make her feel more a part of the gang, if you know what I mean?"

"Your serious?"

"Yep. She lost Robertson and it must be fucking hard for her on her own, when we can die together. I don't mind sharing you until the end. Look. Go and fuck her in the kitchen right now. I'm going upstairs to grab a bit of sleep. After you've had a good session, wake *me* up and fuck me until my clit can't take anymore! Give her a good one Dean – she's expecting you!"

"Game on - Feyer. Yeah I guess I'd better show her round the kitchen! Jeez my cock thought the day of a *double-fuck* was long - gone! Thanks!"

The pair parted with a passionate kiss at the top of the cellar stairs and whilst Feyer went upstairs, Blackwell re-entered the kitchen.

"Hi Claire. I thought that we could fuck all the bad images away for a few hours!"

"Yeah – that sounds cool. Sorry I'm a bit moist already! Feyer told me that you were coming up. Shit – me and my words!"

The pair started to rip each other out of their tattered clothing whilst exchanging tongues with a savage intimacy. Blackwell already had a rampant erection after Feyer's words and Hines knelt down to take his penis in her mouth. She managed to take over half of Blackwell's large cock down her narrow throat and whilst this was ecstasy, he freed himself quite quickly because he wanted to shoot his semen deep into Claire's vagina. The woman had left her skimpy briefs on, but Dean ripped these off and roughly pushed her onto the cold marble - tiled floor. Then the man straddled her and with a deep thrust pushed his penis deep into the woman's vagina. She screamed through sheer lust as orgasmic waves pulsated through her whole being and then she wrapped her tapered legs around Blackwell while he drove into her with increasing speed. The *power* of the copulation had both of them sweating profusely after a matter of seconds and Blackwell's knees started to bleed due to the powerful strokes that he was delivering Hines. His ejaculation lasted for the best part of a minute and Claire lost count of the number of times that she came. Both of them then slumped to the floor on their backs, arms clasped and still breathing heavily. It had been an excellent *bonding session.*

Feyer laughed when she heard the pair thrashing about below her. She didn't feel any jealousy or regret concerning the copulation that she had activated because she had fully meant what she said – in her eyes all three of them were on a metaphorical *death row* and sharing every experience was the order of the day.

Inwardly Feyer was also quite turned on by hearing her lover perform on another woman – before he serviced her.

When Blackwell and Hines opted to go for a second bout of *bonding* she sat on her wide window – sill and gazed out at the harbour. The night didn't have the luminance that was synonymous with the *midnight sun* months, but it was quite light outside nonetheless. She dozed for a short while, before waking to a very *surreal* sight.

A series of retro – gas lamps ran alongside the harbour road and she could clearly discern *snow* falling in the glare created by each lamp. The woman thought about rousing the other two to witness the strange event, but then decided against this course of action and crept out of the rear entrance alone.As soon as her feet contacted the ground, she heard the distinctive sound that footfalls on powdery snow make and she made her way into the large back garden to gain a wider visual perspective.

The woman felt sure that snow in late – August must be down to Klue and she became even more convinced that this weather was the *devil's work* when she took a closer look at the snow that had settled on the ground.

The garden had the same ornate lamps that flanked the harbour and when Feyer moved directly under the beam, she became aware of two very disturbing factors associated with the snow.

The colour of the snow was hardly of the pure – driven white variety, appearing more like a *septic yellow* and it had a distinctive aroma attached to it – comparable with *bad meat!* The woman had seen enough and she ran back into the house.

Blackwell and Hines were oblivious to what was falling outside and their collective sexual groans were even more raucous as they had opted for anal sex on the second time around. Feyer contemplated whether to disturb the pair initially, but then she decided that her *revelation* couldn't wait for anyone. She strode boldly through the kitchen door with a classic entry-line.

"Hey guys, are you ready for a *septic Santa* – check out the poison that is falling from the sky!"

The pair still naked walked over to the kitchen window and looked at the lamplight outside. They could clearly see the snow falling outside, through the glare given off by the lamp and they like Feyer before them were amazed.

Blackwell was very excited about this meteorological anomaly and once again his *boyish enthusiasm* activated before he let *reality* arrest him.

"The electrical storm was fucking weird guys, but this beats that for strangeness. Come on you two, let's go outside – I adore snow!"

"You won't buzz on that batch Dean! It fucking stinks and the colour will really screw up any *picture-postcard*!"

Hines and Blackwell briefly went outside to examine the snow, but like Feyer they returned quite hastily when the smell overcame them. A wind then started to blow the snow around and the yellow flakes seemed to increase in size. Feyer commented on Klue's latest attempt to thwart their Lofoten entry.

"So the bastard wants to trap us in a frozen kingdom guys. He knows that we're coming and I think he fears us. We'll get there though – even if we have to *ram-raid hell* in the process!"

fifteen

The snow fell regularly on Bodo for the next two weeks and it drifted a couple of metres deep in places. The Avoiders remained housebound for the majority of the duration, because the septic nature of the snow was an extremely dangerous health hazard. The elderly citizens who had ventured out when they first saw the snow *fell like flies* and then writhed on the ground in a fatally-determined seizure. Feyer had briefly gone outside to see if she could assist any of those who had fallen, but they were beyond any help.

The pollutant that gave the snow a yellow colour was a sulphur-based compound. Other *toxins* of both natural and *supernatural* origins had entered the atmosphere and Klue's *devil-snow* was the result. The substance was lethal to *anyone* who inhaled it for more than a couple of minutes, if they didn't have a form of respiratory protection.

It was very fortunate for the Avoiders that Claire Hines had brought along a respirator in her survival pack. This meant that the pack could take it in turns to venture outside individually and relieve the tedium of their confinement.

The temperature then dropped quite radically and when the last of the poison fell on September 10, Norway had effectively *surrendercd* to a very early winter! Feyer then managed to acquire more respirators by breaking into a closed medical store and Blackwell prepared his selected boat for their impending crossing. On September 12 Feyer briefly addressed her two fellow Avoiders.

"We will leave tonight – just before midnight. Are you sure that you can get us over in five hours Dean?"

"Yeah, but if the sea becomes rough on the way our journey-time will obviously be extended."

"That's a fair point. Ideally I want you to reach a place called Reine. There's a natural inlet there, where we could scuttle the boat without being noticed. After we've lost the boat, we can follow the coastal path southwards until we reach Hell. It's only about twenty kilometres from Reine to Hell- just a fucking stroll really!"

The Avoiders laughed at Feyer's deliberate humour. All three of them inwardly knew that they were journeying into unknown territory. Feyer's childhood memories might assist them a little, but the devil and his project guns would be waiting for them and in short, their chances of success looked very slim. The three of them had preserved a bizarre *upbeat fatalism* during their time in the house and this had worked to maintain good relations. Though as the clock-started ticking to their departure, the cold realisation of what they were up against started to fully sink in.

Feyer sensed this shift in thinking and ran a check on their supplies to ensure that they stayed focused on their mission. She started by listing their *deadly cargo* first.

"Yo guys - we're going to undertake a final stock check before we load up our boat. Claire you've got *Plutura 26 B* strapped to your back, one machete, the field binoculars and some plastic explosive. Check?"

"Yep. Check Feyer."

"Dean you've got one close-range 9mm pistol,

some steel garrotting wire, one machete, six racked hand – grenades and some manual orienteering gear. Check?"

"Affirmative Feyer."

"Cool. I'll be running with one *beaten to fuck* Uzi, a case of ammunition, a claw-hammer and some acid for close-quarter combat. Check?"

The others checked back and then Feyer continued.

"We've all got to wear the heavy-duty survival clothing that Dean got us from that mountaineering store in Bodo and we've got enough food for a week. We *should* be done before that time has elapsed anyway! Remember the *magic numbers* are 6084277791. Write those fucking digits down on everything that you handle! Now we're going to get some sleep before our journey, but have you got any questions before we hit our beds?"

Neither Hines nor Blackwell had any questions and so the three of them retired to their sleeping quarters.

None of the three Avoiders found it easy to get sleep as their minds were racing with the thrill of their impending confrontation. The *septic-snow* blanket seemed to signify Klue's desperation to Feyer. She wondered if his Lofoten kingdom would be similarly tainted or whether his lair would be as it was when she had visited the place as a child. Eventually her restless mind gained temporary solace from sleep.

Hines had been appointed to wake the others and her rough touch activated a quick response from the sleeping pair. Beads of sweat glistened on the woman's brow due to the adrenalin that was running through her. Hines then spoke the *shared intent* of all three of them.

"Wake-up guys. Time to end Europe!"

The three of them left their temporary home and walked the short journey to the harbour. The respirators made their breathing sound laboured and when they spoke a staccato-echo added an eerie dimension to their words. In a short while the Avoiders located the boat that Blackwell had prepared in readiness for them and after they placed their supplies on the lower deck of the trawler, they climbed up to the cabin. Dean took the central position at the helm and prepared for the passage ahead of them. The powerful twin-engines were then activated and after Hines cut the mooring ropes, the vessel started to leave Bodo harbour behind. As the boat gained power, Claire looked back at the receding land mass and shivered slightly as she thought of the ordeal ahead of them.

The Avoiders were only five kilometres out when the overcast night sky that had been a feature inland, started to clear and they were soon travelling under a very vivid starry sky. Feyer shouted to her fellow Avoiders.

"Okay guys we can lose the respirators until cloud cover returns. It's time for a bit of Arctic-circle freshness in our lungs!"

The sea was incredibly calm; the antithesis of the volatile weather that had dogged the Avoiders since leaving Germany and the waves didn't impede the vessel to any great extent, as it ate up the distance to Moskenesoya. Blackwell was finding it easy to navigate with the charts that were on board and as he plotted a course for Reine, he relaxed a little and concentrated on the aesthetic beauty of the sea reflecting the moonlight.

When the boat was within fifty kilometres of the Lofoten Islands, a dense fog gradually started to replace the natural beauty that they had become accustomed to. Feyer called for the respirators to be

worn again and Blackwell cut the speed of the vessel
down quite dramatically, continuing for a short while
at a miserly five knots. Eventually the fog became so
dense that Dean had no other option but to
temporarily shut the engines down.

As the boat was gently rocked by more robust
waves, Dean activated the digital land – scanning
device that was installed in the cabin. The infrared
system on the scanner calculated that Reine was
twenty-two kilometres distant and Blackwell reported
this information to Feyer. She ascertained if *any* form
of motion was possible.

"You've made great time Dean but we can't stay
drifting like this for too long. If we're still here in
broad daylight we're fucking done for and our bodies
will sink with our lethal cargo before we hit the land-
based spiral winds. It will be a case of *mission failed* –
what can you do?"

"Have a look yourself Feyer. Those massed red
patches between us and Moskenesoya represent rock
clusters. Even if we slow our speed right down, the
chances of not getting holed are miniscule. You see,
there is less than two metres visibility out there and
even the most skilful seaman would probably take this
boat under if they attempted it. It would be
tantamount to suicide."

This further line of *irony* brought the inevitable
laughter from the three of them. Feyer composed
herself and then she spoke again.

"Isn't that what we're about anyway Dean? Look,
if we lose out trying to get through, at least we've
gone down *fighting*, but if we wait for the fog to lift
and are spotted by a project chopper, they'll just take
us out for *sport*! We'd be picked off like flies without
being able to fight back. After all that we've been
through, we deserve to die whilst taking the bastards

with us. We're so close now Dean!"

"So what do you propose then Feyer?"

"I propose that you rev-up this fucker to full power and hit that stretch of water like you're going for a sea-speed record!"

A resigned look came over Blackwell and an exasperated sigh came from his mouth. Then a wry smile registered on his face and he spoke with his *leader* again.

"I had a feeling that you were going to say something along those lines *Ms Deathwish*! Okay then guys – brace yourselves!"

Blackwell then restarted the vessel and soon it was ripping through the water at a maximum speed of twenty – seven knots. All three of the Avoiders stood proud in the half – open cabin as spray skimmed their faces. At first they couldn't see the prow in front of them because the dense fog enveloped every area of the boat except their cabin space. Then after thirty-four minutes, more sections of the boat started to appear in the luminance created by the lights on deck. The fog was lifting!

Hines was ecstatic.

"It's breaking up! Thank fuck for Feyer's nerve!"

When the boat was five kilometres off Moskenesoya, the last traces of the fog disappeared and the coastline could be discerned – stark against the horizon. Despite the temporary halt, Blackwell had made their destination in just a shade over four hours! Feyer flung her arms around him in gratitude, and then she started to help him spot the entrance to the inlet where Reine was located. Initially this proved no easy task, but then Feyer recognised the distinctive Hamney point. This area was just to the north of Reine and now the Avoiders had struck gold.

In the weak, early-morning daylight the vessel was skilfully steered into the inlet and then she was

scuttled in an area of slack deep water. The Avoiders then left the *dying* boat in a plastic life-raft and together, the three of them paddled to the land surrounding Reine. The smell of verdant pasture greeted them when they started to move inland and birds could be heard in the low trees. The scene was a far-cry from Bodo. No septic snow was evident and the respirators were put back in their cases.

* * *

Klue felt uneasy. He could *smell* that his enemy were close and in his rage he visited Wheeler.

"Look at me with your one eye – you fucking idiot! I smell them here Je*ss* – polluting my fetid virtue with their fucking presence. I can't touch *that* woman Wheeler – *you* know that. When we find her I want *you* to personally cut her in half for me. If you manage that, I'll let you keep your sight. The rest of your unit must wipe the others. I have detected only *two* other scents. Even the disillusioned scum who pretend to remain loyal to you can't fuck this up Wheeler!"

"My men have lost their fighting unity Klue. All they've done since we landed is get wasted on Absinth and rape the local women. This place is another party-playground for them. If they could *see you* they would be jolted back in line. I've disciplined the bastards, killed a few of them too, but as soon as my back is turned they're off on another hedonism trip. Couldn't they *see* you?"

"No – not yet. All parties will meet soon head-on. I feel this in my *dead*-blood. Take your men and wait for an ambush along the coast near Sorvagen. I feel right about that region."

"No *pain* today Klue?"

"No I can tell that you are starting to enjoy the pain that I inflict on you. If you *kill the problem of destiny*, I'll hurt you as much as you fucking want."

What Klue had stated had been correct. Wheeler was petrified about losing his remaining eye, but most other forms of mutilation that he experienced at the hands of Klue now gave him a form of psychosexual thrill! He realised this and used it as a dark reward-mechanism.

Wheeler already knew that *the devil* feared Feyer, as the beast had mentioned her place in *prefiguration* before. Klue had eventually told Jess that he could change the call of destiny if he got a human to carry out the deed for him. This meant that Klue subsequently *needed* Wheeler!

The Avoiders spent their first two days on Moskenesoya lying low in the grassland close to their point of entry. Occasionally one of them would undertake a surveillance duty and scout ahead looking over the terrain ahead of them. They moved in a chameleon-like fashion when they were separated from the other Avoiders, blending into hollows with their daubed faces.

Once the scouting was completed the heavy-duty clothing was buried and the tattered rags were put back on. Their weapons were concealed in haversacks and the case was rendered innocuous in appearance with a loose canvas covering. The three of them now looked no different from the inhabitants of Moskenesoya – *at least most of them*!

When the Avoiders entered Reine on the third day, they were surprised to find that this small town was largely untouched as far as the usual overt project *tainting* was concerned. A fish market had attracted a crowd of some size and a few comparatively *jovial* faces were evident. Feyer told the others in hushed tones, that seeing Reine was like going back in time to her childhood days – nothing had changed! Seeing this life of aesthetic simplicity didn't make the three

of them waver in their belief, with regard to what they were attempting to undertake. They knew in their hearts that Europe desperately needed their *coup de grâce*.

A shout went up from the marketplace and Feyer realised that a fortunate opportunity was coming their way. The others not being able to speak Norwegian didn't understand what the man who had made the shout had actually said and subsequently Feyer had to translate his words.

"Guys – good news! The local fishermen are herding a school of Killer Whales along the coastline to Sorvagen. The locals are going to cull them in the shallow water. This act *bonds the community* and folklore is linked with the slaughter. The market traders are going to lay on a couple of transportation lorries to take those people who want to go to the cull. If we go, it will take a few kilometres of our journey to hell and we'll be able to stay unobtrusive if enemy forces come our way. We'll just melt in with the locals."

The Avoiders mixed in with the locals and queued to board one of the lorries. They tightly grasped their haversacks, ensuring that no weapons protruded from them. It was essential that their cover wasn't blown, especially by a trivial mistake! They inched toward the closest lorry and then Feyer stopped momentarily. She was looking at Dean Blackwell who had become transfixed by a piece of paper that was rising in the wind that blew around them. Feyer followed his eyes and together they witnessed the fragment of paper rise upwards in a *corkscrew* type motion. There was no doubt about it – the *spiral winds* were here!"

It didn't take long for the two lorries to make their way up the coast – road to the scene of slaughter. The sight that met their eyes on arrival was gruesome in the extreme, but now the three of them were past caring.

Two Killer Whales had already been forced into the shallows and five burly locals were battering one of the thrashing creatures with harpoons. Blood sprayed high into the air as each blow was struck and jubilant cheers from the locals accompanied each display of barbarism. The Avoiders watched the gory spectacle without saying anything to each other for fear of arousing suspicion from the locals. It was at that moment that Wheeler's cohort arrived to watch the slaughter. Marco Sant had naturally accompanied his leader and it was he who recognised the woman who had caused the MC-Project so much consternation. His eyes had a manic intensity as he informed Wheeler.

"Je*ss*! The fucking bitch is hiding with the locals! Blast the fucker to pieces guys!"

The project cohort started to unleash their firepower in the direction of the local contingent, but the Lofoten Islanders had had enough of their brutality and they readily fought back. Some of the fishermen started to approach the project cohort from the blind- side.

A series of shots ripped the face from an elderly woman, but a local who found a novel way of using his gaff promptly decapitated the man who pulled the trigger! The Avoiders utilised *their* weapons with extreme precision, as ammunition was *limited* to say the least! They cut into the project ranks with close – quarter grenades in the initial skirmishes. When all but one of these had been used, the fight became an extremely savage melee with all three sides cutting into each other less than a few metres apart.

The dying whales still thrashed in the surf whilst their blood ebbed from them. *Human* blood simultaneously flowed down into the shallows –

creating a bizarre fusion in the process. Marco Sant was in the thick of the action. He clocked Claire Hines in the sight of his favoured pistol and then he blew her brain apart! Hardly anything remained of her head and her truncated corpse fell messily into the shallows. He was still on a high from his *kill* when Feyer's claw-hammer smashed into the back of his head. She yelled in vengeance.

"Bleed – you cunt!"

Sant took a few minutes to die. Blood dripped through his fingers as he cradled his smashed head in his hands. This man *deserved* a painful death and Feyer had answered the call.

More Lofoten Islanders joined the fray and the MC-Project forces started to diminish still further. Wheeler's men had experienced countless volatile combat situations, but this was different. Wheeler had told Klue about the general apathy spreading through his men and nearly all of them suffered from delayed reactions that were triggered off by designer drug-addiction. A decade before, Wheeler's unit were untouchable in terms of military prowess, but they had been reduced to fighting clumsily at close-quarters – grappling for gaffs with outraged Islanders! They were effectively paying for indulging in decadent *high-living* for so long. They had lost the edge!

Jess Wheeler fought like a *man possessed* – and in many ways, he was!

He hadn't succumbed to the temptations that had decimated his unit and he used his tall athletic frame to maximum effect. He had discarded his machine gun and chosen to utilise one of the long-handled gaffs as his battle weapon. The man gashed his way through the stomachs of four islanders within seconds of entering the fight and he cast an evil smile in their direction as they bled to death with their guts hanging out. He didn't seem to be impeded by losing an eye and his fighting movements seemed even quicker if anything. The empty eye-socket worked from him in another way – adding a terrifying dimension to his face that froze his enemies. As he hacked his way through the frenzy, he fought with the *chill factor* of a ruthless black zombie and the blood of his victims dripped down his forearms. He turned to seek another victim, but the cards had finally run out for Jess Wheeler!

The man was blasted to the ground when Dean Blackwell threw their last close-quarter grenade in his direction. He hit the ground very hard and suffered acute pain in his face and back. He had also lost the vision in his final eye! The man crawled helplessly across the rough terrain and then the first gaff prodded him – drawing blood on his side. He let out a hollow grunt as his wounds bled more profusely and this meant that more of the islanders noticed his presence. These people *hated* Wheeler, with vengeance glinting in their eyes. In a few days he had been responsible for the deaths, rapes and mutilations of so many of their number – now it was *vendetta-time*!

Wheeler let out a piercing scream as he was *skewered* in the small of his back. Then the man temporarily blacked out in great pain as his left shoulder-blade was punctured. He only lost consciousness for a few seconds though because he was awoken by the *symmetry of pain* that was associated with the piercing of his right shoulder-blade. The final *present* from the islanders involved a sturdy harpoon splicing his genital area. As the battle still raged on around him, Wheeler's evil life started to drain away. The small group of islanders around him still had a *final* form of revenge in store for the MC-

Project leader! They were going to *scatter him to the four winds*! Four long-handled billhooks were put through the wounds made by the gaffs and as the man screamed with terror he was raised on the shoulders of four of the strongest locals. Wheeler screamed for mercy, but he had never shown that quality to others. On a given signal, the four carriers strained every ounce of their strength and slowly started to walk in the four separate directions that they had been given. Wheeler's body was ripped apart in seconds and his *face* was trampled into the dirt.

Fishermen had killed the most powerful man in the world!

Blackwell and Feyer saw Wheeler die and as the battle started to subside with a victory for the islanders seemingly imminent, both of them began to wonder if the passions of these people didn't shed new light on their mission. Neither of them got a chance to re-evaluate their stance though as the *ultimate evil* chose *that* moment to let the world see his presence.

Klue walked from the sea, his plated epidermis glistening in the autumnal sunlight. His frame approached three metres in height and he looked *malevolently* in the direction of the Avoiders. His eyes registered *pure hatred* for Blackwell and a *subdued fear* for Feyer. He drew nearer to the pair, salivating from his cavernous mouth. His ragged hair was ruffled by the spiral winds and Blackwell started to be drawn in by the creature's hypnotic stare. Klue smashed Feyer to the floor and left her reeling. His powerful arm burnt from touching her and he *howled* with rage. With Klue's other arm he then raised Blackwell above his head. The beast walked toward one of the long-handled gaffs and seized it with his burnt arm – proceeding to *thread* the weapon through

Blackwell. The man was in excruciating agony, but he didn't give the beast the satisfaction of screaming. Feyer then came to her senses and unloaded a volley of Uzi bursts into the devil's hide. She recognised the futility of what she had done when the creature gave the woman a *withering* look - almost an act of *black humour* in the context. After Klue had finished threading Blackwell through the gaff, he turned to walk towards the locals who had accounted for Wheeler.

Feyer limped to the side of her lover and he breathed his last in her arms. The *fury* that the woman felt gave way to her grieving and as she cradled the dead body of Blackwell she whispered him a tender lament.

"This will only be a brief parting my love. I never really let you know did I? Know how much I've grown to love you Dean Blackwell-need you-keep you. Our spirits will entwine in hours my love – *death will be our union.*"

As Feyer wept, Klue accounted for the others. Some of them valiantly tried to fight back, but it was hopeless. A fatal yellow fluid was expelled from the creature's mouth and projected in the direction of those who opposed him. When the fluid contacted their skin, it penetrated through to their bones and dangerous fumes were given off in the process. The groans of the dying rose to a new pitch and for a brief moment the sound of the dying seemed to *harmonize* on a low note – like cattle being bled in slaughter. Feyer was unaware of the beast as he walked back into the waves. His stagnant frame disappeared into a *sea of blood.*

Klue couldn't kill Feyer, but he had left a landscape of mutilation in his wake. He swam back to the rocky shoreline of Hell, content in the knowledge that he still had his *black-ace* to play!

THE SCREAM OF FEVER

sixteen

A fetid vapour was rising from the corpses that had been killed by Klue. The scene in front of Feyer had a *damnation* appearance that was similar to the apocalyptic visions envisaged by Hieronymous Bosch.

The woman rose to her feet and her hair was caught by gusts of the spiral winds. She felt that she was in a good place to detonate *Plutura 26 B*, but her mind was set on Hell for the extinction venue. She went over to the mutilated corpse of Hines and undid the knots that tied the case to her body. Then she started walking with the spirit of those who had become casualties on their road. Her act would be *their* prayer and as her feet started to eat up the twelve kilometres to Hell, a faint smile edged the creases of her taught mouth.

The woman stared boldly ahead as she climbed higher up the coastal terrain. The beauty of the landscape around her didn't get registered and her knuckles were white as she tightly held the case to enable European extinction. Feyer didn't feel anxiety or regret, but instead she felt the strength of a person who increasingly come to realise that they could well be following a *predestined* path. She saw herself as a kind of *messenger* appointed by some source higher than her. Of that she was sure and to her death would represent the *start* of a beautiful adventure. If she was

wrong and just a void of blackness lay beyond nothing would exist and thus to Feyer death was a no – lose scenario. She was *content to die.*

When the highest coastal point was reached, the cliff path started to drop downwards in the direction of the derelict settlement known by an infamous name. The Avoider was just under a kilometre from Hell when a woman's voice shattered the equilibrium of Feyer's train of thought.

"Join *us* Feyer – stay in Hell with Klue and I. I am called *Lanz* and I adore serving him. Share my devotion and join us."

The speaker was a beautiful black haired woman with feline-green eyes. She had frankly admitted to being in *league* with the devil from the outset and this factor momentarily surprised Feyer. She had expected that some of Klue's *kind* would approach her as she neared Hell but the beautiful woman had been so direct in her role as *gatekeeper* that for once Feyer had briefly lost the advantage. Those eyes started to *mesmerise* Feyer and she inwardly fought against being drawn in by Klue's handmaiden. She spat back a reply.

"What can *your* kind give me?"

The handmaiden's eyes burned deeper as she twisted the ebony-handled dagger behind her.

"A *clean womb*: pleasure, a clean *new* womb, and children – yes-Feyer children! You can have everything Feyer. You can have as much *pleasure* as you desire: equal status aside his throne, a clean womb, children to nurture and feed Feyer, a life that gives *eyes like mine.* Can you feel their power, do you love their lustre – they could be yours my *beloved.* You would be framed in pleasure – it will be yours for eternity."

Lanz had moved to within a metre of Feyer and

her eyes were sinking their *poison* deep into the Avoider's soul. In a last desperate attempt to resist the temptations of the handmaiden, Feyer flung herself at Lanz who quickly thrust the blade through Feyer's bottom ribs. Lanz smiled in satisfaction as blood started to pump from the Avoider! Feyer then stumbled forward and dropped *the* case to the ground. Lanz saw her advantage and moved toward the case, but this had been Feyer's *bluff-card* and she gave the crouching woman one of the most violent back-kicks that she had ever delivered. It was now Lanz's turn to crumple to the floor. Her blood spattered on the case and the profusion dripped across her broken jaw. Feyer saw that her *enemy* was out for the count and she crawled to her feet again. She staggered on and crumpled to her knees on a small grass mound – just in front of Hell. Her blood had left an intermittent trail behind her and she started to feel nauseous and dizzy. She willed herself on for the *final push*, but initially she couldn't remember the numbers that opened the case! The woman was bleeding to death and becoming increasingly faint – her eyes started to shut! A further gust of the spiral winds blew some of her stomach blood across her face and this served to *revive* her. In a huge effort to remember the combination she spoke out loud.

"Come on now girl for fuck's sake remember! One *last* effort – *608*: For the *others* – *42*, for Dean – my lover Dean *777* and for me – Feyer – *91*! I'm there, get ready Europe – here I fucking come!"

The woman had correctly triggered the case and the lid sprung open. She set the detonation charge and attempted to *stand* for the last time. Klue then started to close in on her position but Feyer saw him and yelled out in triumph.

"Too late you satanic bastard. This is it for you –

174

stay a fucking *prisoner!*"

The wind gusted in the now – familiar *corkscrew* movement and Feyer's hand took hold of the detonator. She thought of Blackwell's smiling face and then she *snarled at the devil.* The woman punched down on the detonator and smiled. As the device exploded thirty metres above her she ended her life with a triumphant *scream - The Scream of Feyer.* Europe started to die – she had won.

epilogue

His cold yellow eyes glinted over the *maelstrom*. He shifted uneasily in his isolation, longing for human souls to torture and move through. He peered across the water, but he knew that no boat would come.

The faintest of smiles started to flicker across his evil face. He could feel the bond between father and sons. He could *smell* the first born in the womb of the *carrier* and as he walked along *his* shoreline, the first *dark name* entered his mind. The first of his three sons would be called *Troth*.

The Scream of Feyer.

By Steve Hammond Kaye

About the author

Visit: www.steve-h-kaye.co.uk

Find *Steve Hammond Kaye, Thirty Four Minutes Dead* **and**
The Scream of Feyer **on facebook**

I started writing *Thirty Four Minutes Dead* in 1990 and concluded the said novel in 1998. I deliberately chose to write the book in a style that is intricate, expansive and visually aware. I wanted the book to engage with the reader in a similar fashion to film on occasions and thus my plot arteries were often determined by a heightened visual perspective.

On the 25th April 2001 *TFMD* was available online for the first time with a publishing company based in Milton Keynes, UK.

Two years later, *The Scream of Feyer* found its way online. This book really is *TFMD*'s *ugly sister* and is a completely different beast. In fact, if it were a animal and you fed it, it would literally bite your hand off!

I wrote this at a time when my life was pretty wild to say the least, so I suppose a strange duality transpired with *The Scream of Feyer* being the mutated offspring.

At the moment i'm writing the third book, *Coils of The Overkill* which will dip-back into the world of *TFMD*. So really, *The Scream of Feyer* must be

savoured as a rare gem of succinct-sickness.

acknowledgements

MS. H. CUNDALL

MS. C. LANZON

MR. M. MARCHAM

MR. H. SLIDELL

MRS. A. M. KAYE

MRS. A. C. KAYE

MR. S. MULLINS

Published by

STANDARDCUTMEDIA
www.publishing.standardcut.co.uk
publishing@standardcut.co.uk

Publishing for the twenty-first century author.

17122493R00106

Printed in Great Britain
by Amazon